"She done it again, Jake!"

She'd run off. Jake looked at his foreman, his heart plummeting. "You going to make me guess, or are you going to tell me?" he drawled with forced nonchalance.

"She rode that crazy horse again." Hank snorted.

"Did she get hurt?"

"Nope. She's one of them fancy-pants riders from back East, ain't she?"

"Could be." Jake shrugged his broad shoulders.

"You reckon she belongs to someone?"

"Could be."

"You sound like a broke record. Don't try to pretend you don't care. You goin' to keep her or not?"

Ellen Rogers drew on her own experience of living in the West and training horses to write *The Lone Wolf*. The working mother of three adult children, Ellen now lives in Ottumwa, Iowa, and says that this last year has been a truly romantic one. She has recently got married *and* sold her first romance novel—*The Lone Wolf!*

To my son, Greg,
"the lone wolf"

THE
LONE WOLF

Ellen Rogers

W★RLDWIDE.

TORONTO • NEW YORK • LONDON
AMSTERDAM • PARIS • SYDNEY • HAMBURG
STOCKHOLM • ATHENS • TOKYO • MILAN
MADRID • WARSAW • BUDAPEST • AUCKLAND

Special thanks and acknowledgment to
Ellen Rogers

ISBN 0-373-83287-7

THE LONE WOLF

Copyright © 1993 Harlequin Enterprises B. V.

This edition published by arrangement with Harlequin Enterprises B. V.

® and TM are trademarks of Harlequin Enterprises Limited. Trademarks indicated with ® are registered in the United States Patent and Trademark Office, the Canadian Trade Marks Office and in other countries.

Printed in U.S.A.

One

A gentle autumn breeze, laced with the crispness of evening, carried the two voices upward to the one pair of ears least intended to hear them.

"You can't do this to me, Brian!"

Kathryn couldn't hear his reply, but hadn't missed the desperation in her sister's voice. Without a moment's hesitation, she turned from the window, gathered up the yards of her white satin wedding dress and ran down the second-level corridor, where she took the back staircase to her father's study. Her hand was on the doorknob when she heard Megan's voice again.

"But you said you loved me. Was that a lie? Did you say it just so you could make love to me?"

Kathryn turned to stone.

"You knew I was engaged to your sister, you little witch. *You* pursued *me,* so don't play the outraged innocent."

"Daddy would kill you if I told him what you've done," Megan threatened in a voice so full of venom Kathryn hardly recognized it.

"I don't think he'd believe you," Brian said. "According to your grandfather's will, it's Kathy who inherits the farm, and by the time she turns twenty-five, we'll already be married. Your father's been grooming me for this job for years, but don't worry. He'll handpick a husband for you the same way he did for your sister."

"I don't want anyone else, Brian. I only want you. I *love* you."

"Then I'm truly sorry, Meggie, but in case you haven't noticed, it's too late."

Nausea swept over Kathryn; her choices were either make a run for it or be sick on the spot. She ran. Her mind remained numb as she fled. She'd nearly reached the stables before she fell to her knees and wretched abominably.

She'd known Brian Conners all her life. In precisely one hour her father was to escort her down the terrace steps to the patio where she and Brian would be joined in holy matrimony under the stars. At this very moment, waiters were offering the guests drinks and canapés. The small orchestra was already tuning up. Only moments before, her father had held her hands in his and told her how proud she'd made him.

She'd known Brian Conners all her life. *She didn't know Brian Conners at all.*

On the terrace, the orchestra began to play, and Kathryn clamped her hand over her mouth to keep from laughing hysterically. Going back now was completely out of the question. Forcing herself to her feet, she stumbled toward the stables.

It would be a while before anyone knew she was missing. The guests would sip champagne and munch on hors d'oeuvres and when it came time for the ceremony wonder what was keeping the bride. Eventually there would be a search. Kathryn's heart beat faster, pumping adrenaline through her veins. She couldn't face anyone to tell them she was calling off the wedding. What could she possibly say? That her own father, a wealthy and respected man, had to purchase a husband for her? That Brian, whom she thought she'd known so well, was a fraud?

Her immediate inclination was to hide in the stables, but that was the first place they'd look. Then they'd search the cattle barns and the house and, last, the old tree house in the cottonwood down by the creek. A sob caught in her throat and she made a dash for the foreman's pickup truck. Gathering up her dress, she climbed into the truck, released the brake and let it coast down the gentle incline. The vehicle fired easily, quietly, and she slipped it into gear. She drove slowly down the lane, then out the front gate.

Almost as if it was meant to be, the gate had been left open. She passed no one. She drove blindly, mechanically. And she didn't feel ... anything.

She didn't actually remember taking the interstate nor did she have any idea how far she'd driven, when the lights from a truck-stop restaurant appeared in the distance, illuminating the inky sky. Out of habit rather than conscious thought, she checked the gas gauge. Oddly, she wasn't alarmed to see that it read empty, or that the vehicle coughed just as she pulled into a row of cattle trucks and horse trailers parked outside the restaurant. She turned off the engine.

Kathryn sat there; it could've been minutes or hours. At first her mind was blank, then slowly, with a strange kind of clinical detachment, she began thinking about betrayal. Her father's. Her sister's. Brian's. The immensity of it all was as unbelievable as the entanglements you usually find only in soap operas.

By now her absence would have been discovered, and a frantic search would be under way. The guests might be cheated out of a wedding, but they'd have plenty of excitement. What would Brian think? Would he be worried, or would he merely envision dollar signs trickling down the drain? And her father? She tried to imagine Iron Man Ryan's reaction and shuddered. Megan, of course, would be delighted if she never returned home at all.

People and vehicles came and went. She thought about just driving on down the highway, but then the fact of the empty gas tank finally registered. She reached for her purse before she remembered it wasn't there. No money, no credit cards, no driver's license. She rummaged through the glove box on the chance of finding a dollar or two, or even some loose change for a telephone call. Nothing. But who could she call, anyway?

It occurred to Kathryn that, as a person, she had no real value. Certainly not to those whose love and affection she'd always taken for granted. She was merely a commodity to be bought, sold, bartered. And she'd never even noticed. She couldn't remember being without financial means or the perks that came with mention of the name, John "Iron Man" Ryan, either. Strip all that away and what was she? Who was she?

A state patrol car pulled into a parking space near the restaurant. As the officer got out and went inside, Kathryn considered asking him for a ride back to the farm. Like a dog slinking home with its tail between its legs, she realized. Distasteful as the idea sounded, it was perhaps her only option. Climbing from the truck, she walked slowly toward the restaurant, the hem of her gown dragging in the dirt. The scent of frying food caused her stomach to churn.

The sound of her own name brought Kathryn to an abrupt stop. A message was crackling over the patrol-car radio. Oh, no! How *could* he? Her father had already called the police! She could just picture herself being dragged back home in disgrace. The runaway child returned to her parent. No, it wouldn't happen that way. She wouldn't allow it. But the final part of the message was a description of the truck.

Kathryn turned and ran to the pickup. Angrily pulling Brian's diamond ring from her finger, she tossed it into the glove box and rolled up the windows as she scanned the parking area for a place to hide. The patrolman was heading back to his car. Had he already heard the message? She sank down in the seat, watching him. Instead of driving off, he sat there sipping coffee from a paper cup. Just her luck.

Kathryn gathered her skirts once again and slipped from the truck. Darting behind cars and semi-rigs, she tried door handle after door handle until she found one that opened. It didn't matter that it belonged to the feed compartment on a long horse trailer. In fact, the familiarity was the first glimmer of comfort she'd had for hours. Fortunately it was empty of animals. She could hide in here, sitting on bales of hay, until the patrolman left. Then she could borrow some change from a waitress and call her father. At least that way *she'd* be the one to make the first move.

Kathryn's head began to spin. *I'd better lie back for a moment,* she thought groggily. And then she fainted.

She didn't want to open her eyes. But the sunlight told her it was time to rise and shine. Besides, Megan was jiggling her bed. "Go 'way, Meggie," she mumbled, rolling onto her side. The jiggling became a bump, bump, bump, forcing a frown to her face. She'd get Megan for this. Kathryn opened her eyes and sat up in one startled motion. Where was she? She blinked rapidly in momentary confusion before the truth came rushing back. The sunlight was coming through a small window of the horse trailer and the trailer was moving! No, it was stopping, tires crunching on gravel. Then doors slammed and she heard voices. She froze.

"You should've woken me, Hank."

"It was a nice night for drivin', boss. No need to bother you. Wouldn't stop now 'cept both tanks are plumb dry."

"So is mine. Let's get coffee and breakfast. I'll take the next leg and you can sleep."

As the voices faded, Kathryn began to breathe again. She waited a long moment, then inched open the door and peered out. Two cowboys, one tall with broad shoulders and narrow waist, the other short, wiry and bandy-legged, were entering a restaurant. Their voices fit them, and she knew instinctively that they wouldn't take kindly to a stowaway. She looked around and a feeling of helplessness swept over her. Where was she? How far had they traveled? This flat, dry, yellowed land was totally alien, but she'd have to make some kind of move, and fast. For one thing, she needed a bathroom. And the coffee and food the big man mentioned sounded like heaven. She realized she hadn't eaten a thing since breakfast the day before. Her wedding day. No wonder she'd passed out.

She started to step out of the trailer, then ducked quickly back inside. A bridal gown would attract attention. Sitting down on the hay, Kathryn tried to decide what to do. If she had scissors, she could alter the gown so it wouldn't be so conspicuous. The hem was already torn. She ripped it further. By the time she was satisfied, two long satin sleeves lay at her feet, plus a considerable pile of fabric from the skirt, but at least her garment looked more like a cocktail dress than a wedding gown. She was reaching for the door handle again when she heard the approaching voices. *Damn!*

"You pull around to the gas pumps, Hank. I'll go in and call the ranch."

"Sure thing, boss."

"Didn't you get enough to eat?"

"Yeah, but I figured we could always use a thermos of coffee, and come midafternoon the doughnuts'll seem awful welcome."

Kathryn clamped her hands over her stomach as it growled, hoping the sound hadn't carried. If she didn't at least get something to drink soon, she'd probably faint again. She thought longingly of that thermos of coffee and doughnuts.

Her chance came when both men went inside the gas station. She slipped cautiously from the trailer, filched the snack, then returned to her hideaway and crouched behind the hay. She was too thirsty and hungry to be ashamed of her actions. She'd pay them back. It wasn't as if she didn't have her own money in the bank. All she had to do was figure out how to get it. She poured out one cup of coffee and wolfed half a doughnut. Not knowing their destination, she didn't dare eat more; she had no idea how long her meager supply had to last.

When the men returned and discovered the missing items, the air was filled with colorful language. One of them even opened the trailer door and peered inside. Crouched behind the hay, Kathryn was sure she'd be discovered, but finally the door closed and they were on their way again. Destination unknown.

Many hours later, she wanted to scream. They'd stopped for gasoline twice. They'd been in and out of mountains and then were entering them again as the moon rose in a star-studded sky. Just as she was seriously considering ripping another piece off her dress to wave as a white flag of surender, the trailer slowed and rolled to a halt. A dog barked. Somewhere horses whinnied. Unmistakable signs they'd arrived.

"Want me to unload the stuff in the trailer, boss?"

"Morning's soon enough. Good night, Hank. Come on, Blue." The cowboy was apparently calling his dog.

"Night, boss."

Kathryn waited until she was sure both men and the dog were gone. Then she slipped out of the trailer and made her way to the stable, which was clearly visible in the moonlight. Horses nickered softly, stomping their feet. Kathryn found a ladder leading to the loft and climbed up, clumsy in her white satin high heels. "Terra firma," she said sighing, as she fashioned a bed of loose hay. Sleep came quickly, but with sleep came dreams, and in her sleep, she wept.

Two

Her cheeks were streaked with tears when he found her the next morning. Now he simply squatted on his heels and studied her. Her breathing was deep and even, and tear-dampened tendrils of chestnut hair curled onto the side of her face. And it was a beautiful face, even if it was smudged with dirt. Her skin was lightly tanned as though she'd spent time in the sun. She looked physically fit, with long shapely legs and slender ankles.

As if she sensed his presence her eyes flew open. Peridot green. The color of his birthstone. He'd never seen eyes that shade before. There was no fear in them, not even surprise. She looked...resolved.

When he spoke he used the same soft voice he used with newborn foals. "You must be hungry."

She sat up and ran her hand through her hair. "I owe you for the coffee and doughnuts," she said simply, quietly.

He said nothing, only watched her.

"Where are we?" she said next. "I mean, what state?"

"Idaho," he answered. "Come up to the house. You'll feel better after a proper breakfast." He stood, offering his hand, surprised when she accepted, though no emotion registered on his ruggedly handsome face. He climbed down the ladder first, then waited for her patiently at the bottom.

She noticed his courtesy and appreciated that he didn't fuss over her just because she was a female, or comment on her ridiculous dress and high-heeled shoes. He must be an extraordinarily sensitive and kind man, for she was, after all, an interloper, and he owed her nothing. It would serve her right if she slipped and fell flat on her derriere. They walked in silence to the ranch house. Kathryn hadn't taken notice of the place last night. This morning she gave it closer scrutiny. A two-story log home with a wide front porch, it fit perfectly with its surroundings.

Preceding him inside as he held the door open for her, she found herself in a spacious living room with polished hardwood floors and a cathedral ceiling braced by wide, sturdy rafters. A huge stone fireplace covered almost one entire wall. The room was designed in a manner befitting male occupancy, with rich, leather-upholstered furniture, but the arrangements of wildflowers on the tables, the lace doilies and pewter frames holding photos of children, suggested a woman lived here, too. But she had no time to dwell on her appraisal.

"You'll want a shower," he stated without preamble. "I think I can find a change of clothes that'll fit you. Take the second room on the right. It's got its own bathroom." He gestured up the open staircase.

While Kathryn showered and washed her hair, she considered her incredible stroke of luck. She could use the rancher's phone to call her father and face the music. It would be easier to do that long-distance. She would ask him to wire money to repay her host for his hospitality. Then she would fly home, at which time she would take on the challenge of facing Iron Man Ryan's wrath, and give Brian a piece of her mind in the bargain.

Then it struck her. She and this rancher hadn't even exchanged names. He didn't seem to care who she was or why she'd stowed away, and apparently felt no need to offer any information about himself, either. Interesting. She found she liked it this way.

A fresh shirt and soft, faded jeans lay on the bed, along with a pair of ladies' undies. Socks and cowboy boots rested on the braided rug. The fit was close enough to be serviceable. He must be married—where else would he have gotten these clothes but from his wife? But where was the woman?

He was waiting for her at the bottom of the stairs. Brunch in the airy kitchen consisted of an omelet smothered in cheese, diced fried potatoes, crisp pieces of fried bread dough. There was orange juice and coffee. They dined alone.

The cook was a petite Spanish woman who, Kathryn sensed, was scrutinizing her carefully. No doubt the woman was suspicious of her sudden appearance and by now had been told she was a stowaway.

As the cook leaned over to pour her employer more coffee, she spoke softly in Spanish, unaware Kathryn was able to understand every word. For hadn't she just spent a year in Spain attending the Dressage Riding Academy?

"Will Señora Jolene be pleased to find you have lent her clothes to a stranger while she is away?"

"Since we don't know when she will return, it hardly matters," the man answered curtly in the same language. Then his voice softened. "We could hardly let our visitor wear that soiled prom dress, could we?"

"Ha!" the cook snorted. "That was a wedding dress, I'm certain."

Señora Jolene, thought Kathryn. Obviously, they were discussing her host's wife. Kathryn kept her eyes on her meal to avoid giving away that she understood what they were saying. His wife's possible reaction wasn't any of her business, and at the moment, she had enough troubles of her own. As soon as she could contact John Ryan and get him to wire money, she would leave. Until that time she would be a gracious guest.

Kathryn almost missed that he had switched to English and was speaking to her.

"I have to ride out and check the mares and foals in the north pasture. Would you like to join me, or would you rather rest?"

Not "can you ride?" but "would you like to?" Did he already know who she was? Had police bulletins reached this far? It was very important to her to contact her father on her own terms if she was ever to gain her independence and the respect she felt she deserved. She had done nothing wrong and would not be treated like a criminal or a delinquent child.

"Is it such a difficult decision?" his deep voice drawled. He was watching her curiously.

"No," she said, meeting the challenge in his tone. "I'd like to see your horses. Thank you for inviting me."

The wrangler she remembered from her trip across country, the one called Hank, had two horses saddled and waiting. Both were bay geldings, one larger than the other. The man acknowledged her with a nod.

"This here's a good-broke horse, ma'am, but he ain't really used to greenhorns. You ever done any ridin'?"

Kathryn glanced over at the "boss," who had mounted the larger animal and sat casually in the saddle with a particularly benign expression. She raised her chin.

Accepting the reins from the bandy-legged cowboy, she swung them over the horse's head. Deftly checking the tightness of the girth with her fingers was second nature, and after doing so she swung lightly into the saddle. Stirrups were the perfect length for Western riding. She usually rode on the smaller English saddles and it had been a while since she'd ridden Western, but the style made little difference for what they were about to do.

"Yep," Hank said almost to himself. "You've rode before."

She glanced at the rancher to find him watching her intently. Without a word, he nudged his horse and moved out, expecting her to follow.

The breeze was soft, warm; it lifted her shoulder-length hair and blew it about in shining curls and waves. Kathryn noticed how he glanced at her from time to time. Did he want to know who she was and what she'd been doing hitching a free ride in his horse trailer? Why didn't he ask? Maybe she should simply volunteer an explanation, but the scenery around them was so foreign, so ruggedly beautiful, all she wanted to do was take it all in and for the moment forget her troubles.

They walked their horses up a hill through a stand of towering pines and down the other side. They crossed a stream that ran crystal clear, gurgling melodically.

"This is a runoff from the Salmon River, fed by mountain snow," he said. "It's one of several that supply the ranch and pasture stock."

"You've never had to worry about your water supply, then?"

"Not as long as there's been a Caulder on this land," he stated with conviction and a touch of pride.

So, she thought, his last name was Caulder. Maybe this was how she'd learn about him. Bit by bit. Slowly.

They crested a higher hill overlooking a narrow valley. More horses than Kathryn could count dotted the knee-high grass—mares and foals against a backdrop of green pines and purple mountains which rose in the distance behind the foothills. The untamed beauty of the vista took her breath away and her eyes almost ached as she gazed around. A lump formed in her throat.

The rancher's saddle creaked and she knew he was watching her again from beneath the broad brim of his hat, his gray eyes questioning. She sent him a tremulous smile. Yes, she liked what she saw, was glad she had come along.

As they moved on, horses abreast, Kathryn began to hear a faint roaring sound. They'd been moving almost steadily upward since they'd left the ranch; as they continued to climb, the sound grew louder. Finally she pressed a finger to her ear.

He noticed. "Come on," he said. "I've something to show you." The glimmer of a smile tugged at the corners of his well-shaped mouth as he wheeled his mount and cantered along the crest of the ridge.

The roar became still louder. Finally he reined in, pointing through a break in the trees. Kathryn moved beside him for a closer look. Far below a turbulent ribbon of water thrashed and raged with unchained power. It was a mesmerizing sight.

"What river is that?" Her words were muted by the noise. "I'd hate to have to cross it," she nearly shouted.

"It's called the River of No Return. You can guess why just looking at it. My great-great-grandfather settled this land. There's been a Caulder on it ever since."

It wasn't a boastful statement, merely a fact. Yet Kathryn heard something in his voice that told her he considered himself an integral part of this land, as much as the rocks and trees and rivers. Generations of sons—but where were his own? Away at school, perhaps? Or with Señora Jolene? Casting a curious glance at him, she tried to guess his age. Mid to late thirties, probably. He looked as wild and untamed as the river below. His tanned features were already etched by the elements, his eyes clear and sharp. His cheekbones were high, his jaw clean-cut. A strong chin. His lips were…just lips, Kathryn told herself firmly. She looked away, back to the river. It didn't seem quite so awesome by comparison.

They returned to the ranch by midafternoon. The cook brought lemonade and sugar cookies, which they shared in the shade of the front porch, flanked by giant pines.

The rancher put down his glass, wiped his hand on the tight leg of his jeans, then extended it to Kathryn. "I'm Jacob Caulder. Friends call me Jake."

Her heart seemed to fall to the pit of her stomach. This was it. Now the questions would begin. Questions she didn't want to answer until later, if at all. She'd been dreading the moment, knowing it would come. Still, she reached out her slim hand and it was completely engulfed in his.

"My name's Kate," she said simply. No one had ever called her Kate, but it seemed appropriate in this setting, and not exactly a lie.

Jake seemed satisfied with her answer, not interested in hearing more. He stood up and stretched. "Well, Kate, I've got some paperwork to do. Maria serves dinner at six. See you then."

Kathryn nodded, barely able to contain her relief.

"And Kate..." his deep voice drawled from the screened door.

She looked up inquiringly.

"I like my women quiet. Try to control that incessant chatter, will you?"

Kathryn gasped slightly, then saw the faint smile curving his mouth. She didn't know what surprised her more, his subtle humor or his use of the term "my women." As the screen door closed behind him, she clutched the cookie in her hand so hard it broke into pieces. No sooner had they landed on the porch than Blue, a speckled dog with a bobbed tail, was there to lap up the pieces. Then he came and sat beside her, cocking his head, asking for more.

Maybe it was foolish not to tell Jake who she was, she thought. If he was willing to take her, a complete stranger, at face value into his home, he was probably understanding enough to let her work out her problems in her own way and not get involved. He didn't seem the type of man to meddle in other people's business. She would call Iron Man just as soon as she figured out what to say.

Kathryn looked down at the pale line where her diamond ring had been. There was only one choice for her. She had to return to Ryan Acres; but it would be only to collect her things and move out. And go where? she wondered. She had no idea. But she had skills. A good accountant could always find a job. Iron Man had convinced her to take accounting in college so that she could manage Ryan Acres' business when she took over. Deep inside, she knew it wasn't what she really wanted, but she did have a good head for figures, as well as a sense of responsibility to the farm.

As for Brian and Megan, they were welcome to each other. Perhaps Brian had never really wanted to marry her, either. Hadn't he as much as said so in the conversation she'd overheard? Her father had contrived the whole thing, chosen her husband as he would choose one for Megan. That sort of thing wasn't done anymore, dammit! Besides, Megan wanted Brian. She loved him.

Kathryn had never questioned John Ryan's decisions before, never opposed him except for last year when she'd begged to go to Spain to study dressage with the experts. It had been her choice of a graduation present. Her father had eventually given in.

She could see the method in her father's madness now. Brian would run the farm, she would be the accountant, and her father would continue to rule his little kingdom until the day he died. He had manipulated all of them their entire lives! The realization made her queazy.

"You must have a lot on your mind." Jake's deep voice interrupted her thoughts. "You've been sitting out here for over an hour."

"I thought you were going to work until dinner," Kate countered.

"I hit a snag with the books. Had to get away for a while. Would you like a tour of the stable? I don't think you saw it properly last night," he said with a faint smile.

"Touché," she muttered as she rose to walk alongside him. Blue followed at their heels.

When they entered the stable, the horses poked their heads over the half doors of their stalls and nickered softly. Jake stopped at each one, giving attention, telling Kate their names and bloodlines as if they should mean something to her. They reached the final stall, but no eager, friendly head appeared.

"Don't get too close to this one. He isn't exactly mean, but he's been in a sour mood ever since I bought him."

Kate could see the animal in the shadowed far reaches of the stall, his face stuck in the corner like a sulking child. He was a huge animal. Something about the way he was built sparked her interest. "What's his problem?" she asked, ignoring Jake's warning and moving closer.

"I haven't had time to figure it out." Jake moved with her, not blocking her view, but keeping himself nearer the stall. Kate noticed the protective gesture and was about to reassure him that she knew what she was doing when he said, "Bought him last month with a couple of brood mares in Amarillo. The owner said the animal was well trained. Belonged to his daughter, who took a sudden interest in BMWs and men. The horse was being neglected. The price was right, and I figured we could always use a big, stout gelding around the ranch. But none of my men can get along with him.''

"He looks bored," Kathryn said.

"Don't know about that. I've got some top riders, though, and he's thrown them all. Hates the saddle.''

Kate shoved her hands into the back pockets of her jeans. "Maybe he's missing his previous owner. Some animals develop major bonds, and if they're sold, will only let men or women, depending on who owned them before, near.''

"I suppose it's possible," he said doubtfully.

"Could we turn him out in the corral for a little exercise? I'd really like to see how he moves." Curiosity about the horse had overcome her shyness.

The minute his eyes connected with hers, she knew he was going to do it; but that didn't surprise her as much as her own reaction to his look. Her heartbeat had definitely picked up in tempo.

The way the animal moved, with a certain fluid grace, made Kate want to confirm her suspicions about his training. There were too many similarities between this animal and the dressage horses she'd ridden at the school in Spain. "Do you have a bridle with a snaffle bit, Jake?''

Kate was watching the animal and she didn't see the muscle clench in the rancher's jaw. "I don't think you should try to ride him, Kate, if that's what you're considering. As much as I hate to refuse, I don't want to see you thrown.''

"I've been thrown before, Jake," she said dryly, bringing her hand up to brush a shining lock of hair from her face. She saw Jake's eyes narrow following the movement of her hand.

"I'll just bet you have," he said softly.

She realized he was staring at the white mark on the third finger of her left hand, and suddenly she understood the double meaning in his words. She blushed.

"Hank, bring us that snaffle Bob uses on the young horses, and Jolene's saddle."

Kate found her voice with his last order. "No saddle," she said firmly, shocking both men.

Jake gritted his teeth. Hank shook his head. But it was Hank who offered his opinion. "We'll be pickin' you up in pieces, ma'am, but it's your neck!"

"Thanks for the warning, Hank. I'll try not to disgrace myself," Kate said with a ghost of a smile. Turning to face Jake, she asked, "What do you call him?"

"We call him a lot of things, but his name is Sinbad."

Jake caught the horse easily and slipped the bridle over his head. As Kate watched, she noticed ranch hands approaching from all directions. Here to see the show, she surmised. Reluctantly Jake gave her a leg up on the massive animal and slowly let go of the bridle.

Kathryn forgot about everything but the horse, who tried a few halfhearted stunts to test her mettle, then gave himself over to the expertise of the light hands on his bit. Soon both of them were engrossed in discovering how much the other knew. Sinbad performed maneuvers on command.

After about twenty minutes Kate slipped from the horse's back and patted his neck. Sinbad reached around and nuzzled her. Hearing an appreciative whistle from outside the corral, she looked up to see cowboys everywhere. Some were still on their horses, having just ridden in from the range for supper. Others were perched on the corral fence. Jake, who'd been leaning on the inside of the corral, walked over, followed closely by Hank.

"Don't that beat all!" Hank exclaimed.

"Hey, Jake," yelled a wrangler. "You never told us you owned a trick horse."

Another, still astride his mount, lifted his hat and scratched his head. "Sure was a purty piece of ridin'. Boss, you better sign her on real quick."

"Don't pay no heed to their teasin', ma'am," said Hank. "Ol' Sinbad here throwed 'em all. But you put on a real good show, and they're just givin' you credit the best way they know how. What was all that fancy sidesteppin' an' sashayin' around, anyways? How'd you get him to do that?"

"I gave him the signals, Hank, but the horse has already been trained to know what they mean. He's a dressage horse." The delight of her discovery glowed in her eyes. "The reason he didn't respond to the cowboys is simply that he's trained to a different set of signals. He's probably never worn a heavy Western saddle and it confused him."

Hank spat a brown stream of saliva from the chew of tobacco that bulged his grizzled cheek. "Reckon I can walk him out a bit," he said taking the reins from Kate's hands. "Maria's probably got your dinner ready, and she hates it when the boss is late."

"Thank you, Hank," Kate said, knowing she'd just made a friend. But it was Jake's approval she wanted, she discovered. She glanced at him, but he remained silent.

Three

Jake reined in his horse when he reached the crest of the ridge behind the ranch, then turned in the saddle as he always did for the view of house and corrals. He remembered stopping like this with his father when he was still just a boy. *Someday the place'll be yours, son. Mind you take care of the land, and it'll take care of you.*

He was committed to the ranch, but it was different now. He kept things to himself—concerns about the future, about heirs. His younger brother, Luke, was well settled in the Caulder logging business. He didn't care for ranching, anyway, wasn't married. His sister, Jolene, had never shown an interest in children; hell, she wasn't that far from being one herself.

He spotted the woman who called herself Kate immediately, brushing her hair at the open window. Red-gold highlights glinted even in the early light of the new day. She wore only a towel knotted at her firm, high breasts. He expelled a long, slow breath that whistled softly through his teeth. She'd slipped into his world from out of the blue, with no explanations. Running from someone. If it wasn't for the profound effect she had on him, he'd hardly know she was around. Unlike Jolene, who was given to frequent displays of temper. He was almost glad in some ways she was someone else's problem now. A congenial peace had reigned at the ranch since her departure. Fewer fights, fewer headaches. It was also boring as hell. At least it had been before Kate showed up.

When Kate left, and he never doubted she would, he'd be left not only bored, but empty. She'd come into his life and fit like the missing piece of a jigsaw puzzle. Like she belonged. He thought about her all day long, couldn't wait to get home to see her and dreamed about her at night. She'd only been there a few days, and yet he couldn't imagine the ranch without her. Maybe, he decided, it was time to do something about her.

It was dusk when Jake rode up to the corral to dismount. Hank came out to greet him. Jake wasn't long finding out what it was.

"She done it again, Jake," Hank said as he lifted his hat in an agitated gesture and wiped his brow with his forearm.

Jake's heart plummeted. She'd run off! "You going to make me guess, or are you going to stop beating around the bush and tell me?" Jake drawled with forced nonchalance.

"She rode that crazy horse again. Didn't even ask." Hank snorted.

"Did she get hurt?"

"Nope. Then she done give him a bath! Combed his mane and tail. Hell, I thought she was even going to powder his behind."

Jake suppressed a chuckle. "Well, there's no law against that."

"She's one of them fancy-pants riders from back East, ain't she?"

"Could be." Jake shrugged his broad shoulders.

"You reckon she belongs to someone?"

"Could be."

"You sound like a broke record. Don't try pretend you don't care around me. I've knowed you since you was knee-high. Are you goin' to keep her or not?"

Jake pulled the saddle from his horse and set it on the corral fence with a thud. "She's not some stray like old Blue there." He nodded at the speckled dog gazing up at him worshipfully. "I can't just decide to keep her."

And with that Jake strode toward the house. He went in and, as his eyes scanned the living room eagerly for Kate, he felt more than a little irritated with himself. That's when he heard the voices from the kitchen and discovered another piece of the puzzle that was Kate. She was having a conversation with Maria, *in fluent Spanish*. He lingered just to hear the sound of her voice.

"He is very angry with her. She has caused him much pain in his heart," Maria said. "I love her, too, but sometimes I think Jake spoils her too much."

"He must really love her."

"Yes. Too much, I think."

"Well, how long have they—"

"Supper ready yet?" Jake made his entrance, and both women turned with guilty looks on their faces.

Maria reverted to English. "Dinner will be ready very soon. Wait until you see what Señorita Kate has made for dessert."

Kate threw him a Mona Lisa smile. "Hello, Jake. I hope you don't mind. I have a foolproof recipe for apple dumplings."

Jake hesitated a heartbeat. "Mom used to make them. I haven't had any since... since then."

Minutes later, as he stood under the shower, Jake wondered if Kate could cook as well as she seemed able to do everything else. In the four short days she'd been on the ranch she'd mastered a horse that buffaloed his best men, made a friend of his dog, had his foreman wanting to keep her, and enchanted his cook. Hell, she was even dressed in one of Maria's favorite outfits. The sight of Kate in Maria's full, brightly patterned skirt, which just barely skimmed her shapely knees, and the off-the-shoulder blouse had nearly poleaxed him. Jake reached for the faucet and turned the water colder.

Kate had noticed that Jake seemed tense during dinner, though he'd certainly done justice to her apple dumplings. Whatever the reason for his mood, be it her presence or his

wife's absence, it was time for her to go. She'd procrasti-
nated long enough. Maybe now that her father had had
some time to cool off he'd be reasonable, or at least willing
to listen to an explanation. Being around Jake wasn't such
a good idea, anyway. It was too easy to get caught up in his
ranch—and in him. Too easy sometimes to forget he was
married. Too hard to forget how the sight of him made her
go all warm inside. She had to leave before things became
more complicated than they already were.

Resigned to the unpleasant task, she climbed off the bed
where she'd been sitting and thinking after helping Maria
with the dishes and slipped down the stairs. A light was
burning in Jake's study. Taking a deep breath, she stepped
to the open doorway. He was so engrossed in his ledgers he
didn't seem to realize she was there.

"My accountant chose a helluva time to go on his honeymoon," he muttered—to himself, she thought. She started
to tiptoe away.

"Are you going to stand in the doorway all night, or are
you going to come in?"

He *had* noticed her. "I didn't mean to disturb you."

"Well, you do," Jake replied quietly.

"I'm sorry," she apologized, misunderstanding. "That's
what I've come to see you about—about my leaving. I realize I mustn't outstay my welcome. You've been very kind,
and when I get home I'll send you a check to cover everything. And now I need to—"

"Come in here, Kate. Sit down. That's the most I've
heard you say at one time since you arrived. Do you want to
tell me about your problems?"

"No. You have enough to worry about. Besides, this is
something I have to handle myself. I need to use your phone
to make a long-distance call. I'll reverse the charges."

"You're going back to him?" Jake's voice held a steel
edge.

"To whom?" Kathryn wondered again if he knew who
she really was.

"Whoever you ran away from in the first place."

Kathryn blanched. There was no use denying it. She wouldn't repay his kindness with an out-and-out lie. "Yes, sort of." It wasn't necessary to add that the only place she wanted to be was *here*.

Jake misread her sudden paleness. "You don't have to go back if you're afraid. If it isn't safe."

"Oh, no, it isn't like that. It's just going to be... very unpleasant."

"It would have to be to make a woman like you pull a crazy stunt like climbing into my stock trailer. It's a damn good thing I was on my way back, or you'd have had a couple thousand pounds of Hereford bull for company."

"That's what you were doing in Illinois? Delivering a bull?"

"Yes. Hank could've done it alone, but I needed to get away for a while. I wasn't sure where you got on board."

"A truck stop outside the Chicago area," she confessed quickly, wondering why he'd felt he had to get away from his beloved ranch. Did it have anything to do with the reason his wife wasn't here? Were there problems with his marriage?

"Kate," Jake said, coming to his feet and leaning over the desk, palms spread wide, "I still want to help."

She wanted to reach out to those broad shoulders and lay her head and her burdens there. The impulse shocked her. "I have to handle this myself—if I'm ever going to have any self-respect... any future, on my own."

"You're determined to go back." It was a flat statement. He could see the affirmation in her eyes. "Make your call then, and don't bother about reversing the charges." Jake left her to make the call in private, but he didn't seem to like it.

She forced herself to dial. Iron Man answered the phone himself. "Kathryn! Have you been kidnapped?"

She shouldn't be surprised at his question. Naturally he wouldn't think her capable of anything so mutinous as running away. "No, sir. I have not."

"Are you hurt?"

Not in a way you'd understand. "No, I'm fine."

"We found the truck, but no sign of you. Your diamond ring was in the glove box. Now you get your butt home, young lady. You've got some tall explaining to do."

"That's what I called about—"

"Right now, do you hear me? You've embarrassed me in front of my friends and colleagues. You've humiliated Brian and damn near broken the boy's heart. Megan hasn't stopped bawling since Saturday night. There won't be another fancy wedding, girl. I'll take the two of you to Judge Evans myself, and by God you'll be married. You can forget that fancy honeymoon, trips abroad and your damned horses, for that matter. You'll shoulder your responsibilities the way you've been taught, and there'll be no more insubordination. Is that clear?" His voice boomed so loudly over the phone Kathryn had to hold it away from her ear. She could almost see his beet-red face and the cords standing out in his thick neck. Her hands were shaking. Not from fear, but from anger.

"Yes, sir, I hear you," Kathryn said through clenched teeth. Then she slammed down the phone and bolted. Out the door, across the yard, to the haven of the stable. Sinbad poked his giant head out to greet her, butting her gently. The tears came then, like floodwaters over a dam, and when strong arms closed around her, she turned in to them.

Jake had seen her dash from the house and followed. He was glad he had. That telephone call had really upset her and she wasn't fit to be left alone. He held her in his arms and she clung to him, letting go the hurt, the tears. She trembled and sobbed, drenching his shirt; he let her cry it out and didn't try to stop her. Hank came into the barn and threw on the lights to find out what all the commotion was about, but when he saw Jake with Kate in his arms, he quickly doused the lights. Jake asked him to saddle his horse. When Kate's sobs eased somewhat, he lifted her into the saddle and climbed up behind her. Holding her tightly, he nudged his horse into a canter across the open meadow.

The wind whistled in her ears, her hair whipping out behind her. The reckless dash through the night suited her mood. It was a wild, reckless ride. She felt the animal's powerful muscles bunch beneath her, then extend as they gathered more speed, racing the wind, running away from pain and sorrow. The meadow was wide, their race long. By the time the animal slowed of his own accord, her tears were gone. They were near a thick stand of pines when the horse stopped, his breathing labored, as was her own. Jake lifted her from the saddle and led her beneath the trees. His arms closed around her, strong and firm. Kathryn felt his heartbeat against her cheek and raised her head, wanting to read his face; but the moon was behind him, splintering through the pine boughs. His head lowered and his lips touched hers, cool and firm, sliding across and back again. Deeper this time, softening as they stroked, tasted. Kathryn's lips parted. A husky sound escaped him as he drew her even closer.

It was not a gradual warmth enveloping her, but a lightning bolt of searing heat that shot through her veins. Hot and wild. Like the ride had been. She was crushed against him, could feel every tight, bulging muscle in his body, yet she couldn't get close enough. She wanted to melt into him. Lose herself in his strength. She twined her arms around his neck, clinging, and kissed him as she'd never kissed any man before. She felt a burning hunger so intense it made her tremble. He cradled her head in one hand, shoving his fingers into her hair, and held on. His other hand stroked down her spine, her hips, pressing her to his body. That same hand traveled to her waist, slid up her ribs and stopped at the side of her breast. Kathryn's gasp was lost in his hungry mouth. She wanted his touch. Her breast swelled beneath his gentle, searching fingers.

She could be his. He wanted her badly. He couldn't ever remember wanting a woman so much. But not like this. Not Kate. She wanted him, too, but in her frame of mind any man might do, and he couldn't stand that. Hell, maybe she was still married! That white band of skin on her finger didn't necessarily mean she was divorced. She might not even realize who it was she was kissing so passionately. He couldn't stand it if she uttered another man's name. His hand slid back to her waist. Slowly, reluctantly, he pulled his lips from hers. It was a painful task, because he hadn't even begun to get his fill. He wasn't sure he ever would.

He felt her withdrawal. Knew she was coming to her senses, having regrets.

"Don't," he said tenderly, pulling her hands to his lips and placing a kiss on her fingers. "It's my fault. I was a fool to get carried away. I want you, Kate, as I've never wanted any woman."

"We shouldn't have done this," she whispered hoarsely. "You're m—"

"Listen to me. I don't know what's going on in your life. You don't have to tell me until you're ready. One thing's for sure—you can't go back. Not yet. You need time to think. Time to heal. You can do that here. He was angry with you, wasn't he?"

"That's putting it mildly," she admitted in a voice that trembled.

"Then stay here. A while longer at least."

"I . . . I can't. What would Jolene say? What would the men think?"

"I don't give a damn! This is between you and me," he growled.

"I have to go back and straighten things out. I can't live this way."

"How can you even think of going back if what you had made you so unhappy, so desperate?"

"I don't intend to stay. I'll get my clothes and some money and then I'll leave. For good."

"And what will you do?"

"I can take care of myself," she said with a slight tilt of her chin. "I . . . I'll think of something."

"Use your head, Kate. What if he won't let you go?"

"He can't stop me." Her voice wavered with uncertainty.

"That settles it, then. You need more time. I've, uh, been postponing a trip to the mountains. We have a line shack up there by a summer pasture where the young stock graze. Young breeding bulls. It keeps them away from the main herd. I need to check on them and I could use some company. You ride well. What I'm suggesting is that you go with me. The land is beautiful beyond description, and I think getting away would help you put things—your life—in perspective."

"Are you crazy? I can't possibly stay with you. That's . . . that's insane!"

"If you're worried about what might happen between us, I—"

"Don't make promises you can't keep," Kate interrupted.

"I don't plan to. I was going to say, it will be entirely up to you if anything develops between us. I've never forced myself on a woman, and I'm sure as hell not going to start now."

"There won't be any problem!" Kate snapped. "I don't go around seducing men."

"I never thought you did," Jake drawled.

Four

It was still dark when Jake walked right into her room and shook her awake. Cripes! she thought. Was the house on fire? She sat bolt upright before realizing she had no gown and clutched frantically for the sheet. "Wh-what is it? Fire?"

"Time to go," Jake replied gruffly.

"Go? Go where?"

"The mountains, remember?"

"Now?"

"Now."

"I thought you meant in a few days."

"Here's some fresh clothes. Everything we need is packed and the horses are waiting. I let you sleep too long as it is. Get a move on." With that, he strode out of her room.

During the quick trip to the bathroom Kathryn splashed cold water on her face, brushed her teeth and somehow managed to remember to take the toothbrush and comb that Maria had given her. There wouldn't have been time to pack any other luxuries even if she had them.

They were already deep in-country when the first pale fingers of dawn caressed the morning sky. Right now she'd have given fifty dollars for a hot cup of coffee. The air was so cold she could see her breath, and she was glad Jake had ordered her to wear the felt Western hat, sherpa jacket and leather gloves. She hadn't planned on this. Not really. She tried to convince herself that the only reason she was here was that he had caught her when she was half-asleep, unable to think up an excuse.

"I shouldn't even be here. I should be placing a call to my bank asking them to send me some money. They'd want identification or I'd already have done it. I'm not destitute, Jake Caulder."

Maybe he hadn't heard her. He was three pack-horses away from her. *Three* packhorses. That translated into a lot of supplies. How long was this trip going to be?

The sun hadn't been up more than an hour before she removed the jacket and stuffed it under her seat. A rotten way to treat his wife's coat, but at least she wouldn't lose it. His wife! If Jolene had any spunk she'd tear a strip off him when he returned. Taking another woman on a camping trip wasn't any way to hold a marriage together.

Kate studied the terrain. They'd crossed too many hills to count, all covered with short, dry grass, their crests ridged with pines that looked like the hair standing up on the neck of an unfriendly dog. Being completely dependent on a man had never bothered her, but that was before she'd come to realize how important it was to be her own person. Before she'd admitted to herself how vital it was to have freedom of choice. Her father had been a dictator. Even her mother... Tears sprang to her eyes, and she refused to finish the thought.

Kate was jarred to her senses when her horse pivoted sharply to avoid the packhorse directly ahead. A less experienced rider would have landed in the creek bed. Jake was watching from the shallow stream where he was letting his horse take a drink. Once on the other side, he stopped, dismounted and waited for her.

"We'll break here awhile. Not too long. I want to make camp by nightfall." After securing the horses, he produced a flask of coffee. Kate accepted the cup he offered before speaking.

"I could have used this four hours ago when I was freezing," she said irritably.

"Then you'll appreciate it all the more now, won't you?"
He poured his own coffee and moved a few feet away to sit
on a fallen log.

Kate cupped her hands around her drink and studied his
profile covertly, wondering how he could look so good after four hours in the saddle. He had removed his hat, and
the sun glinted off his hair. His forearms rested on his thighs
as he cradled the cup in his hands.

A breeze rustled the changing leaves. Red and gold
quaked. His hair ruffled. Birds twittered in the trees and the
stream giggled over its rocky bed as if all was right with the
world. Why was he acting so indifferent? It was his idea she
come along.

"Time to get moving." Jake's voice broke through her
thoughts.

Kate was in the saddle before he could give her a leg up.
She didn't want him to touch her with those strong, sensitive hands ever again. He came over, anyway, giving her an
apple before wordlessly mounting his own horse. They rode
until the sun was well past its high point.

She licked her lips. A drink of water would probably be
too much to ask. And he'd more than likely had Maria fix
him a hearty breakfast before he came into her room to jar
her awake. He could probably go all day like this!

The horses scrambled over loose rock, diverting her attention to more important things, like staying in the saddle.
They climbed the steepest incline of the journey, and at the
top Kate looked down on a wide mountain meadow, teem-
ing with life. Dark red cattle dotted the lush grass. Cowboys were going about their business. Jake led the way into
the camp and up to a row of tents where something smell-
ing deliciously like ham and beans simmered in a kettle over
the fire. Jake swung from the saddle, untied one of the
packhorses and turned him over to the curious man who
came up to greet them. They exchanged a few words before
Jake sprang back into his saddle and, indicating that Kathryn should follow, moved off across the valley, only two
packhorses in tow now.

"Well, that was just dandy," Kate said when they were out of earshot of the camp. "No introduction, no coffee. No lunch. I thought this was supposed to be a relaxing trip."

Jake reined in and turned in the saddle. "We can go back and dine with them if you're that hungry. Personally I don't care for possum stew."

"You're just saying that," she accused. "Aren't you?"

"Nope!" He rode back to where she was stopped and handed her an orange from one of his saddlebags. "You could've let me know you were hungry. At home you eat like a bird."

Home? Kate swallowed past the lump in her throat.

He rode off into the lead again. Kate was beginning to have a little more sympathy for Jolene. Jake was impossible. Who were those men? Whose cattle? Then she realized he'd shown good judgment by not introducing her to a bunch of cowboys; she'd forgotten that the reason she hadn't told him her full name was to maintain her anonymity.

How far was it until they made camp at the cabin tonight? Damn him, anyway. She was getting a little tired of seeing only his broad-shouldered back. He might think he was doing her a favor, giving her time to think; but all he was doing was making her angry. Maybe he was trying to prove he was immune to her. He'd implied it would be entirely up to her if anything happened between them.

"Not likely!" she muttered.

"Did you say something?" Jake called back as he twisted in the saddle.

"Heaven forbid!" she exclaimed dryly. She couldn't be sure, but she thought she saw him smile ever so faintly.

Although no novice to riding, she'd never spent so many hours on horseback at one time. But did he stop to consider that? No. He wanted to reach the cabin by dark. It was nearly dark, at least in the tall, thick pines they'd been traveling through for some time. Damn. She didn't even have her wristwatch. It was back in her father's home, on her dresser along with her money and her credit cards. When they stopped, if they ever did, she was going to bend over and ask her horse to give her a good, swift kick!

Much later, when it was almost too dark to see, Jake reined in by a shallow, rocky stream and uncinched the girth of his horse's saddle.

"Where's the cabin?" Kate asked, still sitting stubbornly astride her horse.

"We might reach it tomorrow if we get an early start," Jake answered without looking at her. He was moving about quickly, hauling packs off the horses' backs and taking the animals to the stream for a drink, rigging the tether line.

"You going to sit up there all night, or come down and gather some dry wood for a fire?"

Kate dismounted stiffly and started to unsaddle her horse.

"I'll do that," Jake said, coming up behind her. "You find the wood. We'll need a good fire to keep the wild animals away."

"You're joking!"

"Bear, wolf, cougar," he said as he dealt with her gear.

She gathered wood quickly, finding plenty in the forest and making several trips. He wouldn't be able to complain she hadn't gathered enough.

"Are you planning to burn down the entire state of Idaho?" Jake said as he came up behind her.

Kate dropped the last bundle and put her hands on her hips. "You said we needed a good fire. By that, I thought you meant big."

"I plan to build a camp fire, not a bonfire."

"So take what you need and ignore the rest. Someone else can use it sometime during the next hundred years." She glanced around her. "If anyone should chance to pass this way again." She thought she saw one corner of his lips twitch as if he was trying not to smile, but it was too dark to be sure.

Jake fixed a package of dehydrated stew, which she ate ravenously. His coffee was dark and rich. It would more than likely keep her awake all night. He had spread her bedroll close to the small, bright blaze of the fire, and when she finally crawled into it, sleep stole upon her immediately, in spite of his coffee.

When he was sure she was sound asleep, Jake slipped a short distance away to wash their dishes in the stream, then, removing his shirt, he doused his upper body in the frigid water. Maybe it would douse his ardor, as well, he thought ruefully. He climbed into his own bedroll and dozed, waking repeatedly throughout the night as he kept watch by the fire. He occupied his mind with questions about her, trying not to stare too long at the indentation of her waist or the swell of her hips as she lay on her side in the bedroll.

It was just as well that she'd snapped at him all day. If she turned into a real shrew it might help him manage his amorous inclinations enough to make this trip tolerable. He should have his head examined for bringing her along. Getting through the day was hard enough, but at night . . .

Kate awakened to the singing of birds and the welcome aroma of coffee. Raising herself on her elbows, she groaned at the stiffness that had invaded every muscle in her body. A thick, damp mist lay over their camp, adding a further chill to the cool air.

She located Jake, hunkered over the fire preparing breakfast. The horses were already saddled, the pack animals loaded. She knew she must have been dead to the world to sleep through all that activity. As she approached the fire he held out a cup of coffee.

"Be careful." He warned. "It's hot."

"Thanks. Need any help with that?" She inclined her head at the skillet over the fire.

"I can manage."

Clearly this was a man who didn't often need help. His eyes were as smoky as the mist, and she wondered what he was thinking.

"You're a pretty self-sufficient guy, aren't you, Jake Caulder."

"A man who isn't doesn't survive out here very long," he answered gruffly.

"Do you always wake up in a sour mood?" She could have bitten her tongue the moment the words left her lips. He was obviously sorry he'd brought her along, even if it had been his idea in the first place.

"What makes you think I'm in a sour mood?"

"You just growled at me!"

Jake rose slowly to his full height and turned to face her. "Would you rather I told you that your eyes are the color of jewels? That your hair is really sexy all tousled from sleep, or that your lips are so pink they beg to be kissed?"

Kate sucked in a breath and stepped backward. "No! I . . . I wasn't fishing for compliments. I—"

"I didn't say this trip would be easy. If you can't take the heat, Kate, don't stoke the fire."

With that ambiguous statement, he returned to his task. Neither one of them spoke again as Jake poured the last of the coffee on the fire and broke camp. Their cautious mood prevailed throughout the morning as the trail wound steadily upward. At one point they passed a forest-ranger outlook where Jake dismounted, leaving her to deal with the horses while he bounded up the steps with a parcel he'd pulled from one of the packs. When the sun was directly overhead they paused briefly to rest the horses, and he doled out dry biscuits and more apples from his saddlebags. Kate gave half of her apple to the bay gelding who had carried her surefootedly on their journey. Both she and Jake kept conversation to a minimum, but the air around them seemed to sizzle with sensual awareness.

Eventually they rounded a bend and began a steady descent along a barely discernible trail through the tall pines. Kate wasn't prepared for the sight that met her weary eyes. A long, narrow mountain meadow opened up to greet them, sheltered on the far side by a sheer, flat wall of rock from which water cascaded to feed the stream wending its way through the center. The cabin itself looked like something left over from another century, its log walls weathered and gray. As they approached, Jake rode up beside her, handing her the packhorses' lead line.

"Stay here while I ride up and check out the cabin," he told her. "We don't want to surprise any unwelcome guests."

Unwelcome guests? She waited nervously as he entered the cabin, heard a metallic banging, then saw a pair of fat raccoons scamper out the door. She smiled for the first time that day. Jake waved at her to bring the horses.

The inside of the cabin wasn't as bad as she'd expected; in fact, it looked cozy. An ancient fireplace was built into one wall. The furnishings were sparse. Utilitarian. A braided rug lay in front of the fireplace. Shelves along one wall held an assortment of cooking pots to use on the small, flat-topped wood-burning stove. Jake didn't ask for help, but began bringing in food, stacking it in a neat, orderly fashion on the shelves. He carried in wood and built a fire in the stove. He brought a couple buckets of water from the pool that had formed at the base of the waterfall, poured some in an iron kettle he'd placed on the stove and set out a washbasin, soap and towels.

"I'll see to the horses while you wash up. Just open the door to let me know when you're finished. Night comes quickly here," he said before he left her alone.

Kate translated that to mean, Don't tarry. When she opened the door to throw out her bath water, Jake looked up from whatever he was doing down by the stream. Minutes later he came in with a couple of trout on a stringer made from twine. He prepared a meal of fresh fish and canned vegetables. Kate watched, feeling useless, thinking how a man as self-sufficient as Jake didn't really need a wife. No wonder he was so blasé about Jolene. A man like this would be a challenge to live with. A woman would be inclined not to feel needed. A sudden vision of herself in his arms a couple of nights ago reminded her of exactly what a virile man like him would need a woman for, and her cheeks crimsoned.

"Something wrong with the food?" he inquired.

Kate, engrossed in her thoughts, hadn't realized he'd been watching her. Her flush deepened. "No. It's very good. My compliments to the chef." She could be blasé, too. "I think it's my turn to do the dishes."

"Fine. I'll see to the horses. I put your clothes on the top bunk. Hope you don't mind," Jake said in a carefully expressionless voice.

But Kate noticed how his eyes scanned her face and came to rest on her lips. "No. That's fine with me."

Yes, everything is just fine! she fumed. She fervently hoped that whatever he needed to do with the young bulls wouldn't take too long, because at this rate they'd soon be at each other's throats. Although she realized the source of his tension she was powerless to prevent it, because she felt equally tense. Pacing around the cabin, she reminded herself he was a married man, even if it seemed to be a strange marriage. If he was *her* husband, she would never want to leave him.

Kate brushed her hand across her forehead as if to erase the errant thought. No matter how much she wanted to feel his strong arms around her or craved the taste of his lips, she could not let herself succumb to the temptation. At times he seemed concerned enough for her welfare to the point of being protective. It was no secret he desired her; and as he'd said on the trail, it was up to her to keep away from the fire.

Five

Kate was beginning to get nervous; Jake had been gone a long time. Maybe he'd been hurt or attacked by wild animals. She didn't know much about the West. She'd never even been this side of the Mississippi before. She paced the dimly lit cabin, straining to hear his return. There was only ominous silence.

Kate opened the door to a crisp draft of mountain air, pungent with the aroma of pine and wildflowers, but Jake was nowhere to be seen. The meadow was bathed in silver-blue light from a full moon, and the only sounds were the wind sighing through the trees and the gurgling of the stream. No planes, trains or automobiles. Just nature in the raw. Untouched, untamed. The sky was filled with brilliant stars, close enough, it seemed, she had merely to reach out her hand to pluck one from the black velvet tapestry. Countless stars in a heaven whose vastness seemed to diminish the earth. How breathtaking this all was. How beautiful.

She had left her shoes in the cabin, but she didn't care as she ran out into the meadow for a better view. With her head thrown back, she turned around slowly, trying to recognize constellations. It was too much for her heart to hold. She danced and frolicked like a carefree child. And there was no one to witness her foolishness. Free! Free! She felt truly free for the first time in her life. Her cavorting eventually brought her near the stream where the stones on the bank put an end to her primitive escapade.

"Ouch! Ow! Ooh!" Between gasps, she giggled as she tried to pick her way closer to the water. Its gurgling laughter urged her on. She wanted to put her toes in to see how cold it was. Moonbeams on the ripples looked like thousands of shiny, new half-dollars bobbing up and down. She wanted to touch, feel and taste everything. To sniff the air that was so crisp, thin and fragrant.

She hadn't sensed Jake's presence, but suddenly there he was, in only his boots and jeans, standing in front of her. His dark hair was damp, raked back by fingers to lie flat against his head. The stubble of beard that shadowed his strong jaw and the silver glint in his eyes sent a shiver up her spine. He looked very formidable, very male. His chest was bare save for the mat of dark, springy hair, and his shoulders were broad, rippling with muscle. "This was a mistake," he said almost savagely.

Kate didn't pretend not to know what he meant. "Yes, it was." The moon-etched planes of his face made him look dark and dangerous, but right now it wasn't him she feared. It was herself. The way her lips craved the feel of his again, the way she wanted the touch of his hands—in spite of everything. He turned as if to step away, then spun back to face her.

"There's just one thing I have to know," he said.

The palpable tension in his deep voice made Kate's heart flutter like a hummingbird. "Yes?" Whatever he asked, she would answer truthfully.

But he didn't ask anything. He swept her into his arms and kissed her hungrily, and as if he might go on forever.

With a sweet wildness singing through her veins, Kate clung to him, trying to fill the emptiness she'd never understood before. She reveled in the hot, smooth moistness of his lips, the roughness of his beard against her fevered skin. She felt his need, his desire, and she wanted him. Wanted him with every fiber of her being. With her heart and with her soul. It was this man her heart had been waiting for. She moaned when he lifted his lips from hers.

"I guess I got the answer to my question," he said huskily as he pried her arms from around his neck.

Kate's head was spinning. She didn't understand what he was talking about. "Wh-what was the question?"

"Are you as passionate when you're happy as you are when you're sad. Yes. You are."

Jake's words hit her like a savage blow. She turned to flee, overcome with humiliation and anger, when her bare foot landed on a sharp stone. An anguished cry escaped her as she stumbled in pain.

Jake caught her before she fell, swept her up in his arms and began carrying her back to the cabin.

"Put me down," she wailed through her pain, both physical and emotional. "Don't you dare touch me. Put me down!"

She kicked her legs and pummeled him with her fists, but to no avail. He carried her into the cabin and tossed her onto the top bunk as easily as if she were a rag doll. Then he proceeded to take her foot and inspect it.

"Just a bruise. You'll get over it," he stated flatly. A minute later he left the cabin, his bedroll under one arm, his rifle under the other.

Kate lay awake half the night.

A blue enamel coffeepot sitting on the stove when she awoke was evidence Jake had returned at some point. When Kate went outside there was no sign of him, and his horse and saddle were missing. The first thought that flashed through her mind was that he'd left her, and for a brief moment she nearly panicked. But Jake was a man who took his responsibilities seriously. He would never abandon her while she was under his protection. She'd stake her life on it.

Returning to the cabin, she noticed the fire in the stove had burned down to a few glowing embers. The coffee was barely warm. She drank two cups quickly before she changed into fresh clothes. His wife's clothes! Was that why he'd pushed her away last night, become angry and insulting? If that was the case, she was glad he had, because she'd completely lost her senses. The realization didn't comfort her long, though.

At last she could bear her thoughts no longer. No matter that the bruise on her foot was still tender, she left the cabin, without any idea where she was going, only knowing she had to get away for a while.

Frustration spurred her on. How had she managed to make such a mess of her life? She'd been an obedient daughter, a good student, a loving sister. She'd been faithful to Brian. Then, on what was supposed to have been her wedding night, her safe, orderly little world had come crashing down around her. From that point everything went wrong. She'd made hasty, irrational decisions and did things that were totally out of character. The question was, what did she do now?

When she finally stopped, and looked around her, the air was so thin she could hardly catch her breath. She had no idea how long she'd climbed, but she was above the timberline, looking down on the meadow far below.

Kate sat down to rest and enjoy the view. The air was a little cool, but the spot she chose against a sun-warmed boulder felt safe, snug. Those were sensations she hadn't felt for years and until now hadn't realized she'd been missing.

When a shadow passed overhead, Kate looked up to see an eagle, wings spread to an astonishing width and hovering on an air current. The fine feathers on its elegant head refracted the sunlight with golden brilliance. Then, with a tilt of its body, it soared off over the meadow. Mesmerized, she sat very still for a long time, watching until it became a speck in the wide, blue expanse of sky.

The mountain seemed to come alive around her. A furry, striped chipmunk darted toward her, stopped and stood on his tiny hind legs. He darted to and fro with nervous energy, trying to determine if she was friend or foe. Soon a bold, sassy bird alighted on a nearby rock, cocking his head sideways to inspect the stranger who'd entered his territory. Deciding she was harmless, he began to preen his black feathers and strut about, scolding the little chipmunk. It was as if the creatures, offering her this show of trust, were accepting her into their world.

Then a movement at the edge of the timber caught Kate's eye. A huge elk emerged from the trees, halted and raised his head to sniff the air. He stared in her direction. She noticed a few points of his antlers had been broken. When his curiosity was satisfied, he turned and walked majestically back into the trees. Kate let out a gasp, and at the sound, the chipmunk darted away and the bird flew off with a noisy flap of wings. Only then did she realize she should be heading back down the mountain. For a short time, though, she'd found peace.

The ground was mostly rock with some thin patches of soil to which delicate tundra clung with surprising tenacity. Kate discovered that going down the mountain was much more difficult than the upward hike had been. Her boot heels kept slipping, and all at once she was gaining momentum, half running to keep her balance. Then a loose outcropping of rock sent her tumbling through the timber like a runaway snowball, end over end, until her descent was finally halted by a sturdy young pine. Kate lay dazed, the breath knocked out of her. Eventually she was able to groan, then after carefully flexing muscles and tentatively moving joints, she decided nothing was broken. When she felt stable enough to stand, she leaned against the tree for a moment before hobbling slowly, cautiously, down the trail.

Jake rode up to the cabin with an uneasy feeling. He shouldn't have left her alone all day. The cabin was empty. The fire in the stove had gone out, and a dreadful weight settled in the pit of his stomach. The little fool wouldn't try to leave, would she? No. Her horse and saddle were still here. Her clothes were still here.

He had to find her. Fear for her safety sent him tearing out of the cabin, searching for her tracks. He found them and mounting his horse, followed the faint indentations of her boots with anxious eyes. She had crossed the stream, dammit. What did she think she was doing? Jake looked across to the far side and saw her limp from the trees.

Kate stopped and looked up at the sound of thundering hooves. Horse and rider came at her with tremendous speed across the shallow creek bed. As they drew near the horse slid nearly to its haunches as the rider leapt from the saddle. Jake's Stetson was pulled low over his eyes, but she could tell by the set of his jaw he was not in a good mood.

She drooped from exhaustion as he strode up to her. His posture could only be described as aggressive. She glanced up at his eyes and grimaced.

Jake glared down at her sunburned face, her hair full of pine needles and her dirt-caked clothes. "Have a nice day, did we?" he growled through clenched teeth.

"I saw an elk! And an eagle!" she exclaimed.

With a derisive snort he swept her up in his arms, carried her to his horse and put her on the saddle. He swung up behind her, and they rode back to the cabin, where he carried her inside. For a long, breath-stopping moment he simply stood there holding her. Not looking at her.

"I can walk," Kate grumbled. "Why do you always have to carry me?" She was too conscious of his strength when he did. Too aware of the magnetism that made her want to melt in his arms.

"Because it feels good," he answered, shocking both of them. Setting her down, he went to the stove, jerked open the door and stoked up the fire. He was very angry.

"I guess the fire's gone out," Kate mumbled to break the tension.

"Not by a long shot," he replied angrily.

Kate frowned, wondering if he was speaking literally or figuratively. "Sorry," she said.

Jake turned to face her. "Where are you hurt?"

"It's just my ribs. Nothing serious." Kate dismissed her injuries with a casual flip of her hand and moved away from him.

"How did it happen?" he demanded.

"I fell. No harm—"

Jake grabbed her arm, turned her around and lifted her shirt.

"Stop that!" Kate hissed.

Despite the fact that she had both of her slender hands around his wrists trying to push his hands away, he proceeded to remove her shirt. "Quit fighting me, Kate," he said softly. "I've got some salve that will help... Oh hell," he groaned as he realized she wasn't wearing a bra.

She clasped her arms around her breasts and glared at him, eyes shimmering beneath a pool of unshed tears. She was defiant, nevertheless. "I want you to leave me alone," she said firmly. "I want to take a bath and put on clean clothes, and I want you to take me back." The speech cost her every ounce of willpower she had, but it was effective.

"I'll bring some water for you," Jake offered stonily.

"Don't bother. I'm going to the waterfall, and I want you to stay away."

"For a woman who doesn't talk much, you sure know how to get your point across."

Kate felt a little better by the time she returned to the cabin. The cold water had been a shock, but it had also helped ease the soreness in her ribs. She ate the stew he offered and insisted on washing the dishes afterward. Jake dried them.

"I've had enough of this," Jake declared. "You're in pain and I'm going to put something on that scrape. Believe me, you're going to feel worse tomorrow."

"Don't you touch me," Kate warned, backing away from him.

"What do you think I'm going to do? Rape you?" he snarled.

"No." He would never do that, but he might easily seduce her.

"Then quit acting like it and get over here." His voice softened slightly. "You don't have to take your shirt off, just lift the hem. You can keep your modesty intact."

Her side was throbbing, and since he put it that way, she decided to comply. He was sitting in a chair at the table holding a jar of ointment in his hand. Kate lifted her shirt, holding it tightly under her breasts. He was trying to be gentle, but still it was painful. "You're hurting me," she said.

"Not as much as you're hurting me."

CLAIM YOUR FREE ISSUE & FREE GIFT! RETURN THIS CARD TODAY!

FREE Romance Magazine!

Finally—the perfect romance magazine for today's busy woman! _World's Best Romances_ fits easily in pocket or purse, and each issue features _four complete romance stories_ by the world's bestselling romance authors.

These are short, passionate love stories, perfect for those occasions when you don't have a lot of time! Send for your free issue today and you'll also get a beautiful gold-tone necklace just for giving us a try!

World's Best Romances is not available in stores, but you can send for a copy with no obligation to subscribe! When your free issue arrives, read one of these wonderful stories and you'll be hooked! If you like our magazine and wish to continue, you'll get 5 more bimonthly issues (making 6 in all) for just $10.96—that's a 33% savings off the cover price, and quite a bargain! Or write "cancel" on the invoice we'll send, return it and owe nothing. No matter what you decide, the free issue and necklace are yours to keep. Either way you can't lose, and we think you'll be glad you gave us a try!

J93001001

NAME

ADDRESS   APT.

CITY   STATE   ZIP

© 1993 HARLEQUIN ENTERPRISES LTD   **Printed in the U.S.A.**

A beautiful free gift for you!

This beautiful gold-tone necklace will add an elegant touch to any outfit! It's yours absolutely free when you accept your free issue of *World's Best Romances!* Hurry—return the postage-paid card right away!

20" in length, jewel clasp

Affix
FREE ISSUE/FREE GIFT
sticker here.

BUSINESS REPLY MAIL

FIRST CLASS MAIL   PERMIT NO. 8353   DES MOINES, IA

POSTAGE WILL BE PAID BY ADDRESSEE

Romances

HARLEQUIN
WORLD'S BEST

Free Romance Magazine Offer

P.O. BOX 11213
Des Moines, IA, 50347-1213

NO POSTAGE
NECESSARY
IF MAILED
IN THE
UNITED STATES

Six

Once again they were swallowed up by the gray mist. They were heading back down the mountain, leaving the cabin behind. Jake's prediction had been accurate. She did feel worse. There was a no-nonsense urgency in every move he'd made since waking Kate and handing her a cup of coffee. Carrying the bare essentials in their saddlebags or strapped to the cantles of their saddles, they were wasting no time. He'd made no explanations, asked no questions. He'd simply said they were moving out. The trip was much faster going down, and for the horses, easier. Jake reined to a halt at the ranger station. The man on duty came out to meet them.

"There's been a rock slide farther down the trail, Jake. You'll have to take the shortcut across the river."

Jake stared up at the ranger grimly. "In that case I'd better leave the packhorses here and send someone back up to get them later."

"I'll put them in the corral," the ranger said. "You'd better get moving."

Jake nodded and urged his horse forward.

Trailing close behind, Kate asked, "Why are we leaving the horses, and what did he mean there has been a rock slide?"

"Just what he said," was Jake's terse reply. "Nothing to worry about."

His whole demeanor was making her worry. The only reason they would leave the horses was if there was some really rough going ahead. "Which river do we have to cross?"

"Just a river."

"Which river?" Kate repeated, raising her voice.

"You pick the damnedest time to be conversational," he shouted back.

Kate ignored his barb. "Why are you so angry?"

Jake turned in the saddle. "I'm not angry, I'm disappointed. I wanted to catch up with the herd."

"What herd?"

"The herd we passed on the way up." Jake kept his horse moving down the trail as he answered her questions over his shoulder.

"Why?"

"Dammit, Kate." He reined in his horse until she drew abreast of him. "Those were my cattle the boys are moving down to winter pasture, and that route would've been easier on you. Now are you satisfied?"

"We can't get to them because of the rock slide?"

"Right!"

When she realized he'd been hiding his concern for her behind all that gruffness, she said, "Don't worry about me. I'm doing f-fine."

His response was just a deep-throated rumble that matched the distant thunder.

The mist had lifted, but the sky was dull, dotted with low-hanging clouds. Kate gritted her teeth to keep from moaning at the constant ache in her side. It had cost her dearly to ask him all those questions, every breath bringing on another shaft of pain. But she'd thought he was angry with her, and if he was, she wanted to know the reason. When was he going to stop and rest? She wanted to ask him that, too, but he'd seemed so upset by her injury that she didn't want to cause him any more trouble.

She was completely dependent on him, and sensing danger ahead, knew there was no one else she'd rather face it with. She might be falling in love with him, but he'd never know it. She lost count of the number of times she'd wanted to touch him since they'd embarked on this journey. She had let her eyes caress him, instead, when she knew his mind was elsewhere.

When she first became aware of the roar, Kate realized how unusually quiet the forest had been all morning. She hadn't even heard a bird twitter. A sense of foreboding settled over her as the noise grew deafening. When they emerged from the trees, she saw it. The River of No Return. Jake rode beside her, took the reins from her hands.

"Hang on to the saddle horn!" he shouted.

Kate stared at him, wide-eyed. "You can't be serious! We have to cross *that?*"

His eyes flickered a brief apology, but his voice was firm. "If there was any other way, Kate, I wouldn't put you through this."

As she clasped the saddle horn in a death grip, she knew the meaning of the word fear. The horses moved deeper and deeper into the boiling water. Jake was downstream of her, holding both sets of reins in his capable hands. Her *life* was literally in his hands. The swirling water was up to her knees now, and so cold it took her breath away. The horses were struggling to keep their footing on the slippery rocks.

Oh, Lord, how deep was it going to get? A few more steps and the water was tugging at her thighs, then her hips. The horses thrust out their heads to keep them above the icy torrent. She could feel the surge of muscles as her horse began to swim. The jerking motion tore at her aching body until she thought she would faint. The saddle had become slickly wet, the river current pulled at her with a power that was terrifying, and her legs were so numb from the cold she was barely able to squeeze them against the bay's heaving sides. All around her the river rolled, swirled and bubbled. Staring at it was making her dizzy and not a little sick. Much more of this and she was going to keel right out of the saddle.

"Don't look at it!" Jake shouted. "Focus on the bank!"

Kate tried, but it only showed her what they had yet to get through. In spite of the horses' efforts they were gradually being sucked downstream. She jerked her head in Jake's direction. He smiled and winked. Either they were out of danger, or he was enjoying this like a kid on a carnival ride.

Her horse stumbled, nearly throwing her as its hooves touched bottom again; but Jake was there to grab her shoulder and set her upright. Meanwhile, the bay regained a strong swimming stride. A few more yards and he found footing in the shallower water, then scrambled onto solid ground.

Kate sat in the saddle, a shivering mass of pain and misery, unaware of what Jake was doing until he wrapped a poncho around her shoulders and lifted her onto his horse. Settling her in front of him, he wrapped his arms gently around her.

Kate sank back against the solid wall of his chest. "My horse..." she began.

"He'll follow, especially after the pet you've made of him feeding him your apples."

"I'm being too much trouble," Kate said weakly.

"Just hang on a little longer, sweetheart," he said against her cheek. "Don't quit on me now."

They rode on forever, or so it seemed to Kate. Crazy thoughts ran through her head. Jake's wife wouldn't return. Jolene had left him because she couldn't stand the isolated life of the ranch. She imagined calling her father and telling him the plan that had come in a flash of inspiration in the mountains. All would be forgiven, he would have what he really wanted, Megan would be happy, and Jake... Jake would discover he needed her. And he had called her *sweetheart*.

Crazy thoughts. Brought on by physical pain and emotional desperation. They had traveled so far. Since the ranger station they hadn't seen another living soul. Not farm nor ranch, nor any domestic livestock. Each time she swayed to his horse's gait the pain racked her side, and if it wasn't for his arms protectively around her, she would have fallen off. She was about to beg Jake to stop when she heard the sound of voices, and they rode into a clearing.

Kate could hardly believe her eyes. Right there in the middle of the vast wilderness was a logging camp. The sky was weeping softly, a light drizzle that hadn't been noticeable in the density of the forest. Work had come to a halt. There were a couple of dozen men milling around a mobile trailer and shelter.

Most of the men came to attention when she and Jake rode into camp. Kate barely noticed. Her eyes had fastened on the trailer and the words emblazoned on its side—Caulder Milling. Filling the doorway was a mountain of a man, a little taller than Jake. The lower half of his face was hidden behind a raven-black beard. As he leapt from the steps and trotted toward them, Kate could see that his eyes were gray—just like Jake's.

But Jake ignored the man as he dismounted and lifted Kate from the saddle in the same manner he would a child, then gently set her on her feet.

"Jake!" the young Paul Bunyan boomed. "I heard about the rock slide on the shortwave. Hank radioed in to say he knew about it, too, and figured you might be headed this way, but he didn't mention you had a kid with you."

Kate was leaning against Jake, who seemed to sense she'd crumble if he didn't keep his arm around her shoulders. Maybe she did look like a kid with her hair tucked under the wide-brimmed hat and her body draped in a poncho that dragged the ground. Among normal people she was considered tall and leggy, but around these giants, she could easily be mistaken for a kid.

Jake didn't contradict the younger man's assumption, nor did he make an introduction. He simply said, "I need to use the truck."

But more than that passed between them. Kate not only sensed it, she saw it in their eyes as they exchanged reins for keys. "Call the ranch. Tell them I'm on my way," Jake said over his shoulder as he led her to the vehicle.

Once inside, Kate removed her hat, shook out her hair and leaned gingerly against the seat with a sigh of relief. The mountain man's mouth dropped open in astonishment.

As Jake put the truck in gear, preparing to drive away, a sheriff's car pulled in front of them and rolled to a stop. "Hey, Jake," the sheriff called. "I just stopped at your ranch. Got a message from Hank. Jolene's coming home tomorrow."

Jake saluted from the brim of his hat, a grim expression clouding his features. Then he reversed the truck and drove around the sheriff's car.

Kate was too miserable to notice the curious stare she received from the lawman. Jolene was coming home tomorrow. Dear Lord. How would Jake explain her presence if she wasn't able to get away before his wife returned? She'd have to call her father tonight and ask him to wire the money. Then she'd impose on Jake, or better yet, Hank, to drive her to the nearest airport. By the look on his face, Jake must be sharing her thoughts.

The rutted lumber road lead to a wider, smooth-surfaced one, which gave Kate a much more tolerable ride. Neither she nor the rancher beside her spoke, even when he pulled up in front of his home. Instead, he sprang around the truck, lifted her gently in his arms and carried her all the way up to her bedroom. Maria followed close behind, a cup of hot soup in her hands. Depositing her on the bed, Jake strode from the room, leaving her in Maria's care without a word. Kate knew his mind was on Jolene.

"You eat every bit of this while I run a hot bath," Maria instructed.

Exhaustion, pain and myriad disturbing thoughts made Kate obedient. Her last, most unsettling thought was of her joyous sense of coming *home* when Jake had carried her across the threshold. It was also her saddest thought.

Once she'd finished the soup, Maria helped her undress, and soon she was ensconced in a tub filled with warm, scented water. Kate leaned back and sighed. A bath was just one of many creature comforts she'd always taken for granted, but never would again. Her life changed when she ran away on her wedding night; but she herself had changed even more in those few days spent alone with Jake in the mountains, and she knew she could never return to the way things were before.

Maria was still in the adjoining bedroom tut-tutting and muttering to herself in Spanish about the ugly scrape and bruise on Kate's ribs. Kate wanted to fall asleep right here in the warm water, but Maria was nearby to ensure she didn't. When a soft flannel knee-length gown was thrust over her head, Kate rebelled.

"I don't want to wear any more of Jolene's clothes."

"This is mine," Maria replied with a perplexed look. "But on me, it reaches the floor." She giggled. "Now, into bed with you."

Kate relented as she stretched out between clean, cotton sheets. "Well, maybe for a short nap." The call to Iron Man could wait for half an hour or so. Closing her eyes, she smiled, hearing Maria still tut-tutting as she slipped from the room. This woman she'd met only a few days ago, who really didn't know anything about her, genuinely cared. Kate counted herself lucky to have made a friend like that.

Kate's last conscious thought was that of the river. She understood now how it got its name. Having experienced firsthand its terrible power, she knew anyone caught in its grasp would be swept away. There would be no return... no return... no return...

Seven

"Kate...Kate..." The insistent voice continued to prod her. *Leave me alone,* she wanted to say. Every muscle, every bone in her body, groaned in protest. The bed moved as a weight settled beside her, strong arms encircling, lifting. Kate cried out, her eyes fluttering open.

"I'm sorry, Kate," Jake said gently, easing her down again. "The doctor is here. I had to wake you."

"I don't need a doctor. What time is it?"

"Nearly seven."

"In the morning?" Kate's voice rose with irritation.

"No. Evening. You've only been asleep a couple of hours."

"I have to call my...uh...I have to make a phone call. I have to make travel plans." Kate struggled to sit upright.

"You're not to move until Dr. Brooks has a look at you."

"Stop being so bossy, Jake. I have sense enough to know if I need a doctor." Kate scowled at him, then noticed the other man in the room.

"I'm Simon Brooks, Kate. Of course, almost everyone just calls me Doc. I'd guess you aren't seriously hurt if you have enough spunk to stand up to Jake Caulder. But why don't you let me take a look at your ribs, anyway. If nothing else, it'll put Jake's mind at rest."

Kate gave in reluctantly, but it was worth it to see Jake's expression when the doctor ordered him out of the room and shut the door firmly in his face.

"Well, Kate, you could have a hairline fracture, but we can't be sure without an X-ray. You've stretched a few muscles farther than they care to be stretched, but nothing seems torn. Most of the discomfort you're feeling is from muscle spasms. I can give you something to ease that, but rest and time are the best medicine. You said something about travel plans. Are you going far?"

"Illinois," Kate replied.

"That's quite a distance. I'd advise you to rest a few days, but I'd probably be wasting my breath. I think you should see your own doctor when you get home."

"I will." Kate smiled wryly. "I guess I'm not in such great physical condition as I'd thought."

"Few of us are." He chuckled. "Jake said you had a fall in the mountains. If you aren't accustomed to them they can be treacherous. He also said you had a tough time crossing the river. I know how that must have upset Jake, too."

Kate remembered how Jake had smiled and winked at her. "If he was afraid, Doc, he didn't show it. He looked like he was having the time of his life. I was the one who was petrified."

"Oh, Jake's not afraid for himself. He almost lost Jolene to that river, and I know he didn't want any harm to come to you."

Jolene. Kate paled at the mention of the woman's name. She was arriving tomorrow!

"Are you allergic to any medications?" Doc asked.

Shaking her head, she mechanically swallowed the pill he handed her, her mind busy with the reasons she had to leave and the method by which it could be done.

"It was a pleasure meeting you, Kate. If I see you again, I hope it's under better circumstances."

"Thank you, Doc," she murmured.

"I'll leave these tablets with Jake. Just tell him when you need one. Try to get some rest."

Rest? She had no time to rest. Just a few minutes for the pill to take effect, then she'd go make that call.

The few minutes she'd planned on stretched to considerably more than a few. She didn't awake until Maria came into her room with another cup of soup, fussing until she ate it all. "Maria, would you please lend me a robe or some clothes? I need to go downstairs to use the phone."

"I will ask Jake if it is all right for you to get up," Maria said as she left the room.

Ask Jake? She didn't need his permission to do anything! He couldn't force her to stay in bed. Didn't any of them realize how important it was that she leave? Throwing off the sheet, Kate got to her feet, making it halfway across the floor before a swooning sensation hit her. At the same moment, Jake burst through the door.

"Where do you think you're going?" he demanded.

"To make a phone call!" Kate snapped.

Scooping her up in his arms, Jake carried her back to bed. "It can wait," was his inflexible reply.

"No, it can't. I have to get out of here!"

"What's the big hurry, Kate?"

"Don't joke about this. When we were at Paul Bunyan's, I heard the sheriff say Jolene will be home tomorrow. How do you propose to explain my presence?" Merely talking was costing her an effort.

"Paul Bunyan?" Jake couldn't help laughing.

"That big man with the beard, and eyes like yours," Kate explained drowsily.

"Oh. Yeah, I guess my little brother does look a bit like Paul Bunyan, but what does Jolene have to do with us?"

Kate sighed as her eyelids drifted down. "You can't be that ... that thickheaded."

She slept, but Jake didn't leave the room. Instead, he pulled a rocking chair up near the bed, sat down and watched her, needing to reassure himself she would be all right. That was where Maria found him an hour later.

"The sheriff is here, Jake," she whispered. "What do you think he wants at this time of night?"

"Hard to say. Tell him I'll be right down," Jake whispered back, as he stood and stretched. He watched Kate's slow, even breathing for another moment, then silently left the room.

"Tate. Must be something pretty important to bring you out this far. What can I do for you?" Jake's voice was brusque, his handshake firm.

"It's important," the sheriff said soberly. "Can we talk in private?"

"Couldn't place where I'd seen her face until I got back to the office. There was a faxed picture of her staring off the bulletin board right at me. It is her, isn't it?"

"It's Kate. Kathryn Ryan." Jake leaned his elbows on his desk looking down at the photocopy of the fax the sheriff provided. "Who the hell is this John Ryan, anyway? Her husband?"

"Don't know. All we got is what you see here. Name, photo and a number to call to collect the five-thousand-dollar reward. I can't understand why you didn't press to find out who she was." Emery Tate finished his coffee and stood. "I'll have to question her, Jake."

"Not tonight, you won't. The doctor sedated her and I'm not going to let her be disturbed." Jake hadn't moved, but his eyes told the sheriff not to press him. "She's a grown woman, Tate. I figured she'd tell me when she was good and ready. I'll talk to her in the morning. I want to hear her side of it first. There has to be a good reason why she fled."

The sheriff rubbed his jaw pensively. "She's listed as a missing person. I'm obligated to report her whereabouts. It's probably too late to do anything about it tonight, but I'll expect a call from you by tomorrow afternoon latest—with her side of the story. Until then, let's just say I'm leaving her in your protective custody, and don't you dare let her out of your sight. If she refuses to tell what this is all about, I'll have to come out and talk to her myself."

"Fair enough," Jake agreed. He shook the sheriff's hand to bind the agreement.

The first sight Kate had when she opened her eyes the following morning was of Jake standing over her, a worried frown creasing his dark brow. The urge to reach out her hand and caress his tanned, clean-shaven jaw was irresistible. As he leaned over her, she did just that. "Jake," she murmured.

"How are you feeling?" he asked tenderly. All the frown lines faded like magic.

"Much better," she replied, still caressing his cheek.

Turning his head fractionally, his lips found her palm and he held them there, his eyes closing as if savoring her display of affection. It was the first time she had ever reached out to him. It didn't matter that she might not be awake enough to use good judgment. She was touching him as she'd wanted to for so long, and seeing both tenderness and passion in his dark eyes. His lips found the inside of her wrist, trailed up her arm, sending tiny shock waves that traveled straight to her heart. He smelled of spicy soap and mountain air, his hair brushing her cheek as he nuzzled her collarbone, brushing aside her gown as he sought the creamy swell of her breast. Kate drew in her breath when his tongue flicked across an eager nipple, teasing it before he took it into his mouth. Her hands clutched at his shoulders as flames shot through her body, engulfing her in their heat.

Kate whispered his name over and over until he raised his head, silencing her with a hungry, possessive kiss. Her arms wrapped around his neck, clinging to him. She wanted this one last kiss. There had been so few, but with each one she wanted him more. Loved him more. It was wrong, yet it was unbearable to think of leaving him, as she must. Even though she couldn't bear to think of him with Jolene, she wouldn't cause another woman the kind of pain brought by betrayal, as she had known. At least now she understood her sister Megan's position, loving one man so desperately you forget about right and wrong. It was a shocking revelation. A sob broke from her throat.

"Did I hurt you?" Jake immediately let go of her, muttering a curse.

"Yes . . . no." How could she explain that the pain was in her heart, not in her ribs, without letting him know how much he meant to her? It was the one thing she could never tell him, because her past was still unresolved, and most importantly, because he belonged to someone else.

"I'll have Maria bring your breakfast," he said, sitting up, his breath coming in gasps as a puzzled frown creased his brow.

"No, Jake. Don't bother. I'm getting up. Just ask if she'll lend me some clothes."

"The doctor said you should rest."

"Please, Jake." She spoke firmly, despite the tremor in her voice.

"I suppose you need to discover for yourself how weak and sore you really are. And you will, once you start to move around. Don't," he said, shaking a finger in her direction, "get out of that bed until Maria is here to help you." With that soft-spoken warning, he backed out of her room and closed the door.

"I hope I'm not disturbing you, Jake, but I need to make an important telephone call. If you have a second phone, I'll be happy to use it so you won't be bothered."

Jake looked up at her standing there in the doorway to his office, rigid with determination, as if expecting him to refuse. "Well, there is one in my bedroom. I'd be happy to take you there."

He let the sentence hang, watching her reaction. It was a cruel thing to do, but at the moment, he wasn't feeling particularly kind. How could she say she'd be happy about making arrangements to leave him? Here she was, determined to go back to John Ryan, when the only place she belonged was at Caulder Ranch.

"You're not disturbing me," he said, finally relenting. "I can't get last month to balance, anyway." He waved his hand over the open ledger on his desk.

"If I get it to balance, will you give me some time alone to make my call?"

Mild shock flickered across his face before he began to smile. "Honey, if you can get this to balance you can have anything you want."

He'd been over these sixteen columns a dozen times, and he couldn't find the error, but that wasn't the point. She seemed so confident, and that was what peaked his interest. "Please, be my guest," he challenged smoothly, offering her his chair behind the desk. "This will probably take awhile," he added pointedly, then called out to Maria to bring coffee.

Kathryn began at once to recalculate the columns, her fingers flying over the adding-machine keys. The tape slithered out across the desk in snakelike fashion. Her eyes never left the row of figures, her fingers never hesitated.

Jake's cocky smile faded. She obviously knew what she was doing. She was so absorbed in her work he could probably stand on his head and she wouldn't notice. Kate had told him once that she wasn't destitute. Odd he should recall that conversation now. He'd taken so much for granted. It was obvious she was well educated, but he hadn't considered that she might have any professional skills. He knew nothing about her. She'd wanted it that way, and he wasn't normally the kind of man who pried into other people's business. Now the time had come for him to find out what she was going back to, because he refused to let her walk into a dangerous situation. He had to be sure she would be safe, and happy.

"Okay. I've found the problem," Kate said crisply. "Come look at this."

As Jake leaned over her shoulder he was hard put to keep his hands off her and his mind on the figures. Her hair was scented like a mountain meadow, and he could see the swell of her breasts under the rounded neck of the peasant blouse Maria had lent her.

"You made an error in payroll deductions here and here—" she stabbed the paper "—then a simple transposition here. You must've had a lot on your mind to make this kind of mess. Anyway, the books balance now."

Jake didn't contradict her. The errors told him that it was his *accountant's* mind that had been elsewhere. On Jolene, to be precise. When Jolene had called from Boise to announce that she and Daniel Wade had eloped, Jake's bellow had nearly raised the roof. But Jolene had hastened to add that she was of age and now a married woman very much in love with her husband. The argument that followed was a painful memory. Dan spoke to him, as well, saying eloping had been a last-minute decision, that the books were balanced and they would be back to face Jake's wrath in two weeks.

Jake was glad he'd had the wisdom to refrain from saying what he was thinking. He'd been hurt that his baby sister hadn't waited for his approval and a proper wedding at the ranch. At least she'd waited until she was twenty-one, but just barely. Jolene still walked with a limp from a compound fracture suffered when she'd taken a daredevil ride in a raft down the River of No Return; she'd nearly drowned, as well. And throughout the year it took for her to recover she'd been a regular little termagant. So, after hearing the news of the elopement he'd decided he needed a change of venue and had accompanied Hank across country to Illinois to deliver a prime young breeding bull. Which, of course, was where he'd inadvertently picked up a stowaway named Kathryn Ryan.

"Did you hear what I said?" Kate was asking. "Do you want me to explain it again?"

"I got it the first time, *Kathryn*. But if you're in the mood to do some explaining, why don't you explain why you ran away from your husband?" Jake leaned one hip on his desk and crossed his arms over his chest.

"How...how did you know?" she stammered.

"Did you think he wouldn't report you missing to the police?"

"But I called. He...he *knows* I'm all right. I am not missing!"

"Apparently he believes you are, and he wants you back. Very much, I might add."

"You talked to Brian?" she squeaked.

"Brian? Who is Brian?" Oh, hell, he thought. Maybe he didn't want to know.

"The man I was supposed to marry."

Jake was floored. This didn't sound like the Kate he'd come to love. He kept his voice level with an effort. "You were running away from John Ryan to marry this...this Brian, but he came after you and somehow you ended up in my stock trailer. Is that the way it happened?"

"No!" Kate shook her head.

"Then how do you explain this?" Jake demanded, showing her the copy of the Missing poster.

Kate gasped, then moaned, clutching her ribs. "Oh. I shouldn't have jerked like that. Big mistake," she panted.

At that moment Jake didn't know which he wanted to do more—comfort her or turn her over his knee. So, bellowing for Maria to bring a glass of water, he handed Kate a pill for the pain, instead.

"That man has gone too far this time," Kate said angrily. "I'd like to wring his neck!"

"There are more legal ways to be rid of your husband, Mrs. Ryan. Have you considered divorce?" Jake said dryly.

Kate's spontaneous laugh bubbled forth, despite the soreness of her ribs.

"I did not intend to be funny," Jake growled as he pushed away from the desk and began pacing the floor, feeling like a fool. "It's none of my business what kind of games you play with your husband, Mrs. Ryan. I just wish you hadn't dragged me into them."

"Oh, Jake, I'm sorry. I didn't intentionally involve you. I did hide in your trailer, but all I remember is getting dizzy, then the next thing I knew we were speeding down the highway. I was so confused and upset I didn't know what to do. I had no money, no credit cards. I didn't even have my driver's license for identification. I was too proud—and too hurt—to ask for help."

"He hurt you? Your husband hurt you?" Jake's voice was deadly quiet.

"I don't mean physical hurt. I mean . . . emotional. And I don't have a husband, Jake. John Ryan is my father."

Relief so great washed over him that he had to restrain himself from crushing her in his arms. It wasn't just that he'd cause her considerable pain but that there were still questions that had to be answered. "Tell me about Brian and that torn dress you were wearing when I found you."

"It was my wedding dress. Brian and I were to be married that night. About an hour before I . . . I overheard something that shocked me so badly all I could do was run."

Her eyes pleading for understanding, Kate related all the details of that horrendous time. Then she leaned her elbows on the desk and buried her face in her hands. "I suppose you're going to have to turn me over to the law now." She looked up again and to his astonishment she wasn't crying, but grinning. Then she giggled. "But first, I'm going to call Iron Man and give him a piece of my mind."

"I think you'd better lie down for a while before you do, honey. That pill seems to be having a strange effect on you." So saying, he picked her up gently and carried her upstairs to her room. She made only the feeblest of protests, and when he placed her on the bed and drew the cover over her, her eyes were already closed and her breathing had taken on the steady rhythm of sleep. He smiled and left the room quietly.

Eight

Jake slammed the ledger shut and reached for the telephone. Emery Tate answered on the second ring.

"Tate, you can call John Ryan and tell him you've located his daughter. Tell him she had a minor accident and is recovering nicely under a doctor's care, but that the doctor advises against travel at this time. He'll want to know where she is of course. You can tell him that, too. And, Tate, there's going to be some trouble on the telephone lines. Don't be surprised if you can't reach me. In case of an emergency, use the shortwave radio."

"Are you going to tell me what this is all about?"

"Nope."

"I didn't think so."

Leaning back in his chair, Jake considered his responsibilities. Caulder men had forged an empire in cattle and timber. The train derailment that took his parents had thrust him into the role of head of the family years ago. He'd shouldered that trust without a second's thought.

Luke, his younger brother, was no longer a teenage football idol, Jolene no longer a heartbroken prepubescent child. But it hadn't been an easy ten years. Luke was now a college graduate with degrees in business and forestry; a born leader, he was a natural to run the logging operation. But at twenty-five he was still breaking women's hearts throughout the territory.

Jolene was the rebel, the wildcat daredevil, who'd dropped out of college after two years, announcing she didn't need any more education to help Jake run the ranch. But the raven-haired, blue-eyed beauty had created a whole new set of problems for her older brother. Many of the wranglers tried to win her attention, and as a result of the competition, fights ensued.

Jake had hired Daniel Wade while Jo was away at college. From Boise, fresh from a broken engagement, the young accountant did his job well and got along with everyone—except Jolene. When she came home the two of them were always snapping at each other. But after the rafting accident, when Jo was confined to the house, things changed between them. Jake knew he should've seen what was happening. He'd known she would marry someday, but he'd never dreamed she'd elope. Not with his accountant.

The truth was it hurt like hell that neither one of them had confided in him. Sure, he would have tried to talk them out of it. But after a reasonable length of time, when he was convinced they loved each other, he would've given them his blessing, along with a big wedding at the ranch.

They were coming home today, and both knew he wasn't pleased. The situation would require his complete attention, and he didn't want to have to worry about Kate, too; for he was certain that calling her father would upset her. So Jake resolutely went about dismantling the internal parts of the telephone. Now there were only four more to seek out and destroy. It would take a couple of days minimum for John Ryan to locate the ranch, but he *would* come. And when he came, Jake would be waiting.

With all of the phones sabotaged so that only he or a repairman could fix them, he returned to his office, opened a wide cabinet and contacted Luke at the logging camp by shortwave radio.

Luella Forsythe owned the only complete women's shop in town. She didn't blink an eye as she tallied Jake's purchases until he selected a half-dozen pairs of lace panties.

"Shouldn't Jolene's new husband be buying these things now, Jake?"

"Who said they were for Jolene?" Jake countered, deadpan.

Lu laughed. "If they were for a lady friend of yours I'd have heard about it. Nothing escapes these ears."

"You seem awfully sure about that," Jake said with a mysterious smile that caused the shopkeeper to scrutinize him more closely.

"I know a couple of ladies who haven't given up on you, but the rest agree you're destined to be a lone wolf. The only wife you'll ever be satisfied with is Caulder Enterprises. Isn't that so?"

"You never know, Lu. Even lone wolves mate eventually," Jake said over his shoulder as he left the shop with parcel in hand.

The drive back to the ranch took a little over an hour. Jake arrived at the same time as the rain. Dan's car wasn't anywhere to be seen in the downpour. He tried to tell himself not to be impatient, but he wanted to get the confrontation over with, their lives back to normal, so he could concentrate on Kate. She was taking up more and more of his thoughts, and his frustration grew each time he saw her, touched her. Where before he'd been satisfied with giving his all to the businesses and his younger siblings, he now wanted—no, needed—something else. He wanted one special pair of green eyes welcoming him home every day. One warm, passionate body sharing his bed. One soul mate. But what did Kate want?

She'd run away from her father and from the man she was going to marry. Why? He knew Kate had grit. She'd proved it on the ride back after she'd been hurt in the mountains, and especially on crossing the river, even though he knew she'd been nearly paralyzed with fear. But she'd never once backed down from what had to be done. She'd showed courage when she climbed on Sinbad's back. And, she'd even stood up to *him* a time or two. Whatever caused her to run must have been pretty damn bad. Jake remembered her kisses. Sweet, honest passion. But then she'd seemed to withdraw. Was she still in love with her fiancé, or had she been so hurt that she was afraid to love?

There was so much he didn't know about her! He didn't have to close his eyes to envision her dancing in the mountain meadow under a full moon, or her face each time she saw a new and wondrous sight. He carried those images with him always, as he did the way she looked after he kissed her. He'd get to the bottom of her problems if it was the last thing he ever did.

Kate was standing by his office window looking out at the rain when Jake came in and handed her the parcel. "The phones are out," she announced dismally. "It must be the storm. What's this?"

"A few clothes. The bare necessities."

"You got them for me? You shouldn't have done that, Jake."

"I know you don't like to wear someone else's, and don't say you can't accept them. I owe you for balancing the books."

"No, you don't, but I'll keep them if you let me pay you as soon as I get back to Illinois. I can send a money order."

"I'd rather you didn't."

"I insist."

Jake shrugged. "How are you feeling?" he asked.

"Terrible." Kate put the parcel on a chair and turned back to the window to watch the rain. It was much easier than looking at him and wanting to throw herself in his arms.

"Oh, Kate," he said sympathetically, placing his hands gently on her shoulders. "Do you need something for the pain again?"

His touch was nearly her undoing. She wouldn't cry. She wouldn't. "That's not the problem, Jake. I need to make arrangements to fly out of here. I'd wanted to be gone by now. The phones aren't working, so I can't reach my father to tell him to call off that ridiculous missing-person report."

"That's been taken care of, so you can relax."

"You called ...?"

"No. Sheriff Tate notified him that you'd been found."

Kate spun around, paying for it with a sharp pain in her side. "That's just great! Twenty-five-years old and I'm being treated like a runaway adolescent." She shrugged off Jake's hands and paced across the room. "I wouldn't go back at all if I didn't have to collect my things," she fumed.

"Now you *are* acting like an adolescent."

"Thank you. I really needed to hear that."

"Sarcasm doesn't become you, either."

"It's hardly fair for you to judge me when you don't understand the circumstances."

"You've never told me what they are, Kate," Jake admonished.

It was an invitation to confide in him, to cry on his big, broad shoulders about how she'd been wronged. Did she really want to explain how Brian had succumbed to an infatuated younger woman, or how her little sister had tried to thwart her wedding with last-minute pleas of love? Did she want him to know how her father had plotted her marriage to a man he could control? No. Jake might feel sorry for her if he knew. And that was the last thing she wanted from him.

"You're right," she said decidedly. "I was being childish. Now if you'll excuse me, I'm going to put these clothes in my room and then help Maria with dinner."

Kate had been on tenterhooks all day expecting Jolene to come barging into the house in a jealous rage, demanding to know what this strange woman was doing there. Kate dreaded angry scenes, and she'd planned to avoid the coming one by pleading a headache as soon as they'd finished their meal—but by then she didn't have to lie. Along with the headache came the spasms in her side. Declining medication, she settled for a long soak in a hot bath before crawling into bed to listen to the rain drumming on the windowpane.

Nine

In that supernatant state of consciousness between dreaming and waking came the sensation of being watched. More tangible was the patter of rain against the window. A voice nudged Kate's senses, not a voice she recognized. When her eyes drifted open, she saw a young woman, a beautiful raven-haired young woman, standing beside her bed holding a steaming mug.

"So you're the one who's got Jake all in a tizzy," the stranger said.

Kate blinked, unable to find her tongue, not knowing what to say if she did.

"I'm surprised we didn't wake you. I brought a cup of coffee so you'll be braced if you decide to join the melee downstairs. I'm Jolene, but you probably already figured that out." The young woman leaned over, studying Kate. "You look a little dazed. I guess you're not awake yet. See you later."

Not awake? Who was Jolene kidding? The dazed look was shock. Kate clutched the quilt around her throat as Jolene, despite her slight limp, strode impressively from the room.

How many ways were there to die? Kate wondered. Embarrassment, humiliation, mortification. Guilt. But it wasn't as if she and Jake were lovers. All right, he had kissed her and she had kissed him.... Kate moaned. She was such a fool. Obviously Jake had mentioned her to Jolene, but what had he said?

That was the question that prodded her to scramble out of bed and into her clothes—the ones Jake had bought her. They weren't a gift. She intended to pay him for them as soon as she could. His selections were practical. Jeans, Western-cut blouses, socks, a pair of tennis shoes. Mind you, the lace undies were a bit much.

By the time she combed her hair and brushed her teeth the coffee was barely warm, but she gulped it down, anyway, wondering afterward if it had been laced with arsenic.

The morning was darkened by the rainstorm as Kate came down the staircase to see Jake, his wife and another man sitting in front of a brightly burning fireplace. The scene would've been cozy if not for the expressions on their faces. Jake's was like a thundercloud, Jolene's rebellious and the other man's comically chagrined. All three heads turned in her direction to stare. The tension disconcerted her, so that she said the first inane thing that came to mind. "What time is it?"

"Six o'clock," Jake replied with an odd half smile.

"In the evening?" Kate said, astonished. She'd been keeping weird hours since her mishap.

"Morning. You had a good night's sleep for a change," he offered, his smile widening. To the others he explained devilishly, "Kate has this problem with night and day when she first wakes up."

Kate felt her cheeks flame. He made it sound as if they'd been sleeping together. Why was he doing that? Why deliberately antagonize his wife?

"You've met Jo," he went on to say, "even though I told her not to disturb you. And this is Daniel Wade, my accountant."

Both men had stood when she'd entered the room, and now Dan offered his hand. "It's a pleasure to meet you, Kate. I owe you for cleaning up the mess I made of the books." Kate accepted his hand, nodding dumbly. She was grateful for Maria's intervention to announce breakfast was ready—although she wondered how anyone could think of food at a time like this, much less eat any.

There were eggs, bacon, sausage, biscuits, pancakes, fried potatoes, juice and coffee. It made her stomach churn just to look at it, but the others tucked right in.

"Be reasonable, Jake." Jolene was apparently picking up the thread of their previous conversation as if there'd been no lapse. "I didn't do it to hurt you. I've always wanted to be married in a quaint little church in the city. It was all my idea. I didn't want a long-drawn-out affair at the ranch. Dan's father isn't well enough to travel. Luke is too busy wrapping up his logging season, and you're scrambling around getting the ranch ready for winter." Jolene stopped long enough to chew a forkful of food. "I know you, Jake. You would've found a dozen reasons why Dan and I should wait to be married. Frankly, I didn't want the hassle."

Kate was in the act of buttering a biscuit she didn't really have the appetite to eat when her hands froze. *Jolene was married to Dan?*

"I've tried to be more than just the head of this house, Jo. When did I ever hassle you?"

Kate knew Jake well enough to hear the pain in his deep, soft question. *Jolene was his sister!* She was the little girl in the old photograph in the living room.

Kate felt her heart leap with hope as its great burden of guilt was lifted. Jolene's response brought her attention back to the conversation.

"I'm not finding fault with the way you've run the ranch, Jake, or the way you've tried to be a father to me. It's just that, well, sometimes you're a bit overzealous in your responsibilities. Maybe you don't realize it, but there are times that you're an island. Remote, solitary. You keep things to yourself. You're a strong man. You've had to be. But I'm twenty-one now, and may I point out you are not my father."

"The honor of the responsibility for you was thrust on me when our parents died," Jake returned. "It wasn't a job I chose. I did the best I knew how, and gave you everything you wanted, within reason."

Kate was getting dizzy as her eyes bounced back and forth between the two, willing them to come to an amicable conclusion. Sipping coffee to ease the lump in her throat, she wished she could fade into the woodwork, rather than hear this deeply personal family discussion. Jake was either oblivious to her discomfort, or he didn't really mind airing the family laundry in front of her. At the moment, she was painfully aware of being an outsider. Jolene was becoming agitated and Daniel Wade's face was turning red.

"I want a little house in the suburbs close to a school. I want to join the PTA." Jolene warmed to her theme. "I want neighbors to come over for coffee. I want *civilization*. Dan's father isn't well at all. His mother needs us. Dan has been offered a fabulous job in Boise."

"If you wanted civilization, why didn't you stay in college?" Jake growled. "What happened to 'I want to help you run the ranch, Jake'?"

"Come on, Jake. You don't need me for that. You don't really need anyone. You never have, or you would've been married by now. I was just a pain in the neck and you know it. There's Maria to do the cooking and cleaning. Luke is on his own now, and you can hire another accountant just like that." Jolene snapped her fingers. "So don't try to make Dan feel guilty about leaving his job," she added defensively.

Dan was pushing his food around on his plate much as Kate was doing. "I didn't look for the job, Jake. It just fell in my lap while we were in Boise. I hadn't realized Dad's health was slipping so badly. Lord, I felt so guilty for not going back last Christmas, but I wanted to be with Jolene. And she didn't want to leave you alone on Christmas." Dan took a deep breath and faced Jake squarely. "I love your baby sister . . . my wife. I promise you I'll always take good care of her."

All eyes turned to the big, powerfully built man at the head of the table. "I'm sure you will," Jake said dryly. "And probably live to regret it. I doubt you've witnessed the full force of one of her temper tantrums yet."

"I've mellowed," Jolene interjected haughtily.

Kate's mind was still playing back the phrase, *or you would've been married by now,* over and over like a scratched record.

"Kate...Kate, are you okay?" Jake's voice finally penetrated.

"Uh-huh," she said.

Jolene chuckled. "She doesn't talk much, does she?"

"How can anyone get a word in with you around?" her husband drawled teasingly.

When it seemed the situation couldn't become more complicated, the back door swung open and Paul Bunyan filled the doorway, dripping rain. He tore off his boot-length slicker and pointed a finger at Jolene. "I'm going to turn you over my knee and give the seat of your pants the dusting it deserves," he roared.

Jolene's eyes grew wide. "Don't you dare lay a hand on me, you big ox. I might be pregnant."

Everyone froze. Somewhere a clock ticked loudly.

Jolene shrugged. "Well, I've been married eleven and a half days now. It's entirely possible, you know."

Paul Bunyan pulled out a chair beside Kate and sat down. "I'm Luke. My brother, the barbarian, didn't see fit to introduce us the other day. I wouldn't want you to get the impression all of us are crude. How are you feeling?"

"Fine," Kate replied cautiously.

"Those cute little ribs healing, are they?"

"Yes, thank you." She glanced quickly in Jake's direction to see him glaring at her as if she'd just said something he didn't approve of. Well, how else could she answer his brother? The big bear had turned into a playful cub, stroking his ebony beard, his eyes dancing teasingly. He was just trying to be friendly.

"You know, Katie, you have the most beautiful green eyes I've ever seen in my life." Luke smiled, showing perfect white teeth. Maria set a place and a cup of coffee in front of him and Kate passed the biscuits.

"Honey?" Kate inquired politely.

"Yes, my love?" Luke replied, leaning toward her and wiggling his eyebrows.

"I mean, do you want honey for your biscuit?"

"Oh." Luke feigned innocence. "Darn. No, pass me the preserves, please. Honey drips on my beard and the bees chase me for days. Can't ever eat honey."

Jolene snickered, Kate giggled and Jake scowled. Luke had managed to defuse much of the tension that hung over the table. Kate realized Luke was the peacemaker of the family. But a quick glance told her that the thunderclouds were still in Jake's gray eyes. What was the matter with him? Didn't he realize what a wonderful family he had?

"I hear you're quite an equestrian," Luke continued.

"Where did you hear that?"

"Don't be modest. Your fame has spread since you tamed that man-eater."

Kate shook her head. "Sinbad's a pussycat, and he's a very well-trained animal."

"Only in the right hands," Luke said. "I wouldn't mind if you took a notion to tame me, either."

Jake passed a fresh plate of hotcakes to Luke. "Here, put something else in your mouth besides your foot."

"Oh, gosh," Jolene crowed. "You actually rode Sinbad? Jake let you?" She threw her brother a perplexed look. "I've got to see him, Kate. Come on, let's you and I walk down to the stables."

They put on slickers and were about to leave when Jake stopped them. "Kate," he warned. "No riding."

"Yes, boss," she replied dryly before showing him her back. Damn him, always giving orders. Before she'd ever even *seen* him she'd heard Hank calling him boss. Now she knew why. He was bossy with everyone. Naturally he had a lot on his mind with his sister eloping and his accountant leaving, but couldn't he lighten up just a tiny bit?

"We can be a little overwhelming as a group until you get used to us, but we're not nearly as wild as we appear," Jolene was saying. "Give us a chance, Kate. Give Jake a chance."

"A chance for what?" Kate asked innocently. They reached the shelter of the stable, shedding their rain gear, before Jolene replied.

"Are you trying to tell me there isn't something going on between you and Jake?"

"How could there be? We only met a few days ago. I...I was stranded and he helped me. Anytime now my family will arrange transportation home. But I plan to reimburse Jake for his hospitality."

"Oh, wow, that'll send him into orbit. Kate, you don't pay for hospitality. Not out here in God's country. It would be...well, it just isn't done. You can only repay hospitality in kind, or with friendship and loyalty. It's never offered with any thought of reimbursement."

"Well, I won't have a chance to do that, so he'll have to settle for money. There *are* times when it's appropriate."

"Look, I don't know what's going on, and I guess it's none of my business, but it's obvious to me my big brother is possessive where you're concerned."

"No. You're mistaken," Kate denied emphatically.

"Didn't you notice the look on his face when Luke was plying you with his Caulder charm? Jake was jealous."

Jake—jealous? "No, I didn't. I was still trying to recover from the discovery that you weren't Jake's wife."

Jolene's smile broke into a hearty laugh. "Wife? Don't I wish he had one. Many have vied for the title, but he's never taken any of them seriously. He's given his all to the ranch, to Luke and I. Sometimes I'd see him standing on the porch at night just staring at the stars. He looked so lonely. I asked him once why he didn't get married, and he laughed it off, saying he guessed he was just a lone wolf. Well, the word spread, and the name stuck."

Jolene sighed and crossed her arms in front of her, a frown creasing her forehead. "You know what I think? I think Jake felt he couldn't take the time to get involved. And it would take time for a courtship, because Jake would never marry a woman he didn't love. He's a quiet man, but his feelings run deep. Funny how I can see him more clearly now that I've found someone to love."

"Jake is a very self-reliant man," Kate said, mostly to remind herself. She couldn't afford to get her hopes up.

"But that was all before Luke left home to take over the logging operation, and I got married. Don't you see, Kate, he's ready to settle down now. I'd bet on it. And he *does* need an accountant. Lord, he'd have to be blind not to see how perfect you are for him."

"I . . . I already have a fiancé. Or rather, I *had* a fiancé. I haven't seen him since . . . I came to Idaho. So please don't try to match me up with your brother. As you said before, if he'd wanted a wife, he'd be married by now."

Oh, Jake, she thought. Those little terms of endearment—all of them—that slipped so naturally from his lips had meant nothing. Not even his kisses. It was just a physical thing, though at the time he'd been so convincing she'd let herself believe it might be more. And all the time, she'd been falling in love with him, thinking it was his marriage that made it impossible. Now she realized it was Jake himself. He had the normal desires of a virile man, but he didn't really *need* a wife.

"So, are you and Dan going to live in Boise?" Kate asked with false brightness.

"Yes. You can see why we want to, can't you? I'm not the only one with family, but mine are young and strong. Dan's parents aren't." Jolene's voice quivered, betraying her previous attitude of confidence.

"You don't have to feel guilty for wanting to live your own life," Kate stated. She meant it. Jolene had run away, eloped with the man she loved; but she'd come back to face her family and try to mend the rift between them. That was what Kate had to do. The sooner, the better. Her heart had leapt when she'd discovered Jake wasn't married, only to plummet again at Jolene's words. Jake was a lone wolf, even by his own admission. When they'd been alone together in the mountains she'd felt the raw intensity of his desire. He had said she should get away for a while and think things through, rather than return home, even though he could only guess at her situation. Almost immediately, he'd begun to regret it; and finally, she'd understood why. She remembered the night by the stream and shuddered to think what might have happened had she not believed him to be married and found the strength to say no.

"Kate," Jolene was saying, "it's too bad neither of us is staying here. I'm sure we would become good friends."

Kate nodded, forcing a smile that faded when she saw Jake's familiar silhouette in the open stable door.

"If you're trying to get chilled to the bone, Kate, standing in a drafty barn on a cold, rainy day is the perfect way to do it," he scolded, striding purposefully toward her.

"It isn't that cold," was Kate's exasperated reply. Didn't he realize he shouldn't be showing concern for her? It only encouraged her hopes and made her love him more. It was too easy to tell herself he really did care for her, might even be falling in love with her. He wouldn't try to stop her from leaving once he knew she was fit to travel, or he would have said something to make her stay. He certainly hadn't offered her the job as his accountant.

Taking the slicker from her hands, Jake wrapped it around her shoulders, and it was all she could do not to lean against him. "Maria's made mulled cider. A welcome home for the bride," he added to Jolene.

"Maria's an angel," Jolene said. "Come on, Kate. We'll have a real old-fashioned hen party." Then for Jake's benefit, "Poor Maria. When we both leave she'll be the only woman on this lonely place."

Ten

Kate discovered the phones were working again while Jake was outside saying goodbye to his family. Hurriedly, she dialed Ryan Acres, letting it ring ten times before giving up.

Damn! What do I do now? she wondered. Hank had taken Maria into town for groceries. They'd be gone all day. In a moment Jake would open the door and it would be just the two of them in the big log house. She didn't think she was prepared to handle the idea, let alone the fact.

Her qualms were needless, however, for Jake didn't return to the house. She caught a glimpse of him riding off toward the south pasture where the herd of cattle had been relocated. She had the whole house to herself. Even empty, it felt like home. Sun streamed through the windows, and a brisk breeze stirred the big pines in the front yard.

When Jake failed to return for lunch, Kate went to the stable, turning Sinbad out in the paddock for exercise. She wanted to take one last ride on the fabulous animal before she left, but she didn't dare risk Jake's disapproval. Finally she returned Sinbad to his stall and tried to call the farm again. No answer. She made a hot cup of tea, helped herself to a couple of cookies and sat on the front porch wondering if something was wrong.

By midafternoon, when there was still no sign of Maria and Hank, she decided it was up to her to start dinner. Helping Maria, she'd learned the kitchen well, and now, finding a freshly thawed roast in the refrigerator eliminated the problem of deciding what to fix. She garnished the meat with potatoes, carrots and onions, placed the lot in a pan and popped it into the oven. Then she swept pine needles and dust from the porch, tried another call to Illinois with the same non-result and finally took a bath. Naturally the phone chose that moment to ring.

Venturing forth with a towel wrapped around her, Kate followed the sound, hesitating outside Jake's bedroom door. "This is no time to be timid," she reminded herself. Answering Jake's bedroom phone made more sense than trotting downstairs in just a towel.

The phone was on his bedside table, ringing insistently.
"Hello?"

"Kate! Thank heaven we reached someone. This is Hank. Listen here. There's some problem on the road outside town. A rock slide, the sheriff says. Nobody can get through the north road. You tell Jake that Maria and I are stuck here till sometime tomorrow or at least till they get that blasted rock off the road. Tell him we've got rooms at Mrs. Murphy's boardinghouse. I had to act fast because a lotta folks are gonna be stranded here, too. There ain't no hurry to give him the message. Just tell him when he comes in. Don't be ridin' that fool horse out to find him."

"Okay, Hank. Tell Maria not to worry about the boss's dinner. I can cook. And, Hank, you guys be careful."

After hanging up, she wondered why she'd advised him to take care. Maybe for the same reason he'd told her not to ride out to find Jake. Tears sprang to her eyes. Dammit! The longer she stayed, the harder it was going to be to leave.

She looked curiously around Jake's room. It was definitely a man's room. No frills, no plants. The bed was a big four-poster. A big bed for a big man. A dresser, chest of drawers, two nightstands and an antique rocker filled the rest of the spacious room. And that was it. There were no signs of memories, hopes or dreams. Not even a painting on the wall. He slept here, that was all. It was the den of a lone wolf.

Jolene's room had been different. After their hen party the other day, Maria and Kate had helped her pack. There was memorabilia everywhere. Photo albums, old toys, school pennants, a special rock, an eagle feather, an elk's tooth, a dried, pressed corsage, even a small trophy for winning a local cutting-horse contest. All these things spoke of a life filled with treasured memories. Kate sighed, went to get dressed and then went downstairs.

The roast was browning nicely. She deftly peeled apples, then mixed oatmeal and brown sugar for a crisp dessert. If Jake was late coming home everything would be well done or warmed over, but at least he would eat.

When she was done, she stepped out onto the wide front porch, breathing the pine-fragrant air. An artist's spectrum of variegated blues washed the evening sky, from midnight in the east dissolving to pale turquoise in the west, where the colors transformed miraculously to the dusty rose and peach hues that were all that remained of a sun bidding farewell to day. A long strand of gunmetal-gray clouds hung suspended above the black silhouettes of trees.

A dark horse and rider, backdropped by twilight, loped across an open field of tall grasses bowing their slender shafts to the breeze. Jake sat tall in the saddle, broad shoulders and narrow hips in perfect symmetry with his mount, and as she watched him Kate was sure her heart would break. Lifting her arm in a wide, sweeping arc, she waved. Horse and rider changed course, veered away from the stable toward the house.

He was the essence of her heart's desire. A love she never knew she craved until they met. If he would take her in his arms, she thought, her body would cling to his and her lips would not be still for words of love.

Jake swung down from the saddle and moved up the steps to stand before her. For a breathless moment they stood, transfixed. One sound, one sigh, might have found them in each other's arms. But then his horse nickered and the spell was broken. Kate licked her lips and told him about Hank's call.

Jake nodded. "Then who's cooking dinner?"

Kate sniffed the air. "Uh—oh. I am," she said, dashing into the house.

Jake ate appreciatively, at the same time noticing how absorbed she looked. The heat that radiated between them across the table didn't seem to faze her the way it did him. He was aware of it engulfing him each time their eyes met. Her culinary skills were yet another surprise.

"I didn't know you could cook," he said casually, the corners of his mouth curving up in the way they did when he was teasing.

"All farm girls can cook," she quipped.

"I can't imagine you as a flatland farmer, milking cows and slopping hogs."

"Good, because I never have. We raise Limiosins."

"Now that, I can see. You riding around in a limousine." He chuckled.

"Oh, please. It's a breed of cattle. They're very large and quite beautiful."

"I know what they are." He grinned. "But I can't remember ever hearing a woman refer to cattle as beautiful."

"Then you haven't met the right woman." Kate bit her lip. "I didn't mean that the way it sounded."

"When you're right, you're right," he admitted softly, then changed tack when he noticed her body go tense. *Easy does it,* he reminded himself. "So, really, who taught you to cook?"

"My mother, of course."

"Do you come from a large family?"

"No. There's just my sister and me."

"Don't you think your mother has worried about you during your little escapade?"

"We lost Mom eight years ago," Kate replied quietly. *Fool!* But how was he to know? He had to drag every piece of information out of her. What did she have to be so secretive about? Why couldn't she talk about her family? She wasn't the only one in the world who had problems, but the longer she kept them bottled up, the harder it was going to be to face them. "I'm sorry," he said. "I know how tough it is to lose a parent."

"Yes," she agreed.

"What about your sister? Are you close?"

"We used to be."

Something fleeting in her eyes told him to be careful. "How is it a Midwestern farm girl rides Eastern style?"

"My mother's family were from Virginia. Grandmother was a horsewoman—riding with the hounds and all that. My mother preferred dressage. She met Dad while she was employed at the Pentagon and he was working his way up the military ladder. They were married—and voilà."

"That doesn't explain how you ended up on a farm in Illinois," Jake prodded.

"Grandpa Ryan wasn't pleased his only son wanted to 'play soldier.' His farm was one of the largest in the state, very successful. When Grandpa became too ill to run it, Iron Man Ryan had to return home to save the family fortune. I was five years old when we moved from Virginia, and Megan, my sister, wasn't even a twinkle. Mom gave up her job when I was born, but she never gave up her horses. She brought them to Illinois with us and taught me to ride. And that's how I came to be a farm girl who rides Eastern-style. But in all fairness, dressage is popular everywhere," she added succinctly.

"Thank you for enlightening this ignorant cowpoke," he said with mock humility.

"You're anything but ignorant," Kate said dryly as she realized she'd been cleverly duped into telling him practically her entire family history.

Countless stars filled the sky. They seemed to simply hang there, glowing solidly, eclipsing even the moon. Through the open window of her room Kate heard a lone wolf give its plaintive call. A song, almost. A serenade.

The air was chill, but the shiver running up her spine had nothing to do with the breeze. She strained her ears, listening for the answering call, saddened when none came. The stars became a blur as tears filled her eyes to overflowing. Wind in the pines whispered her name. Kate...Kate... Kate...

"Kate?"

She turned.

"Kate?" A soft, husky whisper.

"I'm here," she answered.

Jake walked toward her silently on bare feet. As he approached, the light shining through the window moved up his body like a spotlight. More and more of him became visible. Snug jeans, bare chest with an inverted triangle of curling dark hair, the strong line of his chin. Gray eyes reflected the moon, silver bright, mesmerizing in their intensity.

"I knew you were awake," he said hoarsely. "I thought maybe you were in pain."

I am, she thought. *But not the kind you think.*

She sighed, then turned back toward the window. His hands closed gently over her shoulders, his breath stirred her hair.

"What are you doing?" he murmured.

"Watching the night...listening to the night. Thinking." Let him think she was crazy. Just don't let him hold her, or she'd be lost.

"You're thinking." His warm breath caressed her ear. "What about?"

"How beautiful it is...here." A shudder rippled through her slender body. Warm, strong arms enfolded her, drew her close.

"You're cold."

She didn't dare deny it or she'd give herself away. For it was him. His touch. His clean fresh scent that made her tremble, her heart ache.

Reaching around her, he closed the window, and turned her toward him. Resistance fluttered and died. Lifting her in his arms, he carried her to the bed. "You mustn't get chilled," he said huskily.

Her heart beat in her ears like a thundering stampede as he laid her down. The weight of his body creaked the mattress as he gathered her in his arms and whispered her name. Feather-light kisses closed her eyes, brushed her cheek, teased the corner of her mouth. Like a willow bending toward water, she sought him out. His lips were firm . . . and stoking.

How quickly he warmed her. Kate's limbs felt like melting butter. Sparks shot through her veins, her body reveled in his touch. Her fingers explored the tautness of his arms, the flat, muscled plane of his stomach, the soft, curling hair on his chest, discovering the wonder of his male nipples, peaked like her own. He shuddered under her caress, and as a sigh escaped her, he deepened the kiss. His hands were gentle for all their size and strength, touching places that kindled the flame of desire into a conflagration. His name hovered on her lips.

"I won't hurt you, my sweet Katie," he murmured against her ear. "I've needed you, wanted you so much."

Wanted . . . needed, the lone wolf cried; but he never sang of love. Kathryn's body tensed. "Don't."

His grip tightened reflexively, causing her to wince. Abruptly he let go. "Why?" he demanded.

Her mind was crawling with memories of betrayal. "Principles," she said frigidly.

A derisive snort. "They weren't evident a second ago, Kate. What turned you off?"

"I'm not a faucet." Her voice cracked.

"I didn't think you were a tease, either."

She started to say something, changed her mind. "If you say so. Now, please, go away and leave me alone."

Jake considered a moment. "I don't think so. What the devil did that SOB do to you?"

"Who?"

"Brian!"

Kathryn covered her face with her hands. Brian was a lifetime ago, ancient history, and yet the memory of her blind gullibility haunted her still. His deceit had had the power to hurt her before she even knew the meaning of the word love. How much more easily and more deeply could Jake break her heart? She knew if she gave herself to Jake for one night, she would never be whole again after they at last said goodbye. He was married to the ranch. His lover, Caulder Enterprises. He didn't need a real, flesh-and-blood wife. An occasional woman would do, and there were plenty willing, she was sure. But as Jake put it, he wanted . . . he needed. She was available.

Kate flew from the bed, and across the room, her diaphanous cotton gown swirling behind her. Then his words stopped her. Spoken softly, they held a ring of truth.

"There's no place to run, Kate. You'd only be running from yourself."

"How perceptive you are, Jake Caulder."

"You're too young to be bitter, Kate." Jake rose leisurely from the bed and went, not toward her, but to stand silhouetted against the window. "I talked to the sheriff today. Your father will be here tomorrow. Brian is with him. They're coming to take you home."

"No!" The word escaped before she could stop to think about it. A purely emotional reaction, but a telling one.

"I thought that was what you wanted. It's all you've talked about for days." He spoke quietly, without sentiment.

"Not like this. Not with Brian."

"You hate him that much?"

"No. I don't hate him at all." Until that moment she hadn't realized it was true.

"What do you feel for him, then?"

"Nothing." She hesitated thoughtfully. "Well, sorry, maybe. I'm more disappointed in my own lack of judgment."

"Are you sure you don't love him?"

"I'm very sure." *Because I love you and no one else.*

"He must love *you*. He's coming." It was a flat statement.

Her laugh held no humor. "No, he's merely protecting his interests. You see, I inherited Grandfather Ryan's farm. Not Father, or Megan. It was a stipulation of Grandfather's eccentric will. He didn't trust his little soldier boy to keep the farm in the family, so everything went to me with my father as conservator, reaping a generous percentage of the annual profits as long as he remains in that position. Brian has been groomed to take over since he was fourteen. He began working for us when his own parents lost their farm to the bank."

"It doesn't sound to me as if you needed to become an accountant."

"Iron Man's brilliant idea. Someone had to do it. Why not me? I had a good head for figures, and I wouldn't have to be paid a salary. It would also keep me tied to Ryan Farm. Brian is a good farmer, but he has no head for managing money. Iron Man is conservator until I turn twenty-five, in two months. I guess I knew all along he resented me because of the will, but until recently, I never knew how much."

"Brian won't let you go easily. Greed is a powerful drive. He stands to lose too much."

"He prefers Megan," Kate admitted. Finally it was out. She'd said the words aloud, and now that she had, it didn't matter. None of it mattered.

"That's what made you run," Jake said with understanding. "You'd been manipulated and deceived."

"You're right. That's what made me run, Jake, and it kept me from making a terrible mistake," she confessed.

"So what do you plan to do now?"

"I'll confront Brian, go home. I'll soon be able to sign the ranch over to Iron Man. A good lawyer can smooth it all out, I'm sure. I don't want any part of the game Grandfather played with his son. My father gave up his dreams of a military career, and he worked hard on the farm after Grandfather died. He deserves compensation for all that."

"Then what?" Jake wouldn't just let the subject of her future drop.

That depends on you. Kate hugged her arms around her
and shrugged. "I'll live my own life. Away from them. It's
Meggie I'm really worried about. She's always felt left out,
and she's so young she doesn't know what she wants."

"You said the farm was one of the best in the state. You'd
give all that up to be free?"

"The minute I made the decision to leave, I was free. I
finally realized what I needed to do, but I was afraid to
confront them all for fear Meggie would be hurt. And I still
know there'll be an ugly scene."

"When did you decide?"

"When I was in the mountains with you. I felt like an eagle there, soaring above all worldly cares, seeing only what
was important. But I wasn't sure how to go about it until we
got back to the ranch and I had time to think."

"You've been through hell, yet you can dance like a child
under the moon. You can smile and laugh and forgive. You
find pleasure in things other people pass by. Like the whisper of the wind, an eagle in flight, the sight of snow spar-
kling on a distant mountain peak. You're fresh and vibrant.
You love it here, Kate. You belong here."

What was he saying? She dared not read any special
meaning into his words. "Well, I probably will settle here
somewhere. Wherever I can find work."

Was that what he had in mind, persuading her to be his
accountant? If it was, she'd given him the perfect opening,
though it had just slipped out. In fact, she'd talked too
much. Why didn't he go back to his own room and leave her
with at least a remnant of her pride?

Jake heaved a mighty sigh. "If you come over here beside me, I'll tell you the story about Blue, and how he came
to be an important part of this ranch."

Oh, great. Now he was going to tell her a bedtime story.
If she listened politely, maybe then he would go away. With
a careless shrug that belied her inner turmoil, Kate obliged.
At least a kind of peace had settled over the room, and him.

"He was a gangly pup when someone dumped him on the
road, half-starved. I suspect he'd even been abused. I picked

him up and brought him home. Gave him food and shelter. I never chained him or put him in a pen. He's always been free to leave, but I guess he's decided to stay. We have an understanding that's based on trust. I consider him mine. He thinks I belong to him."

Kate smiled gently. "Yes, he certainly does."

His face, etched in starlight and shadows, softened. "It was a beginning. We built on that, and it's turned out to be a good, solid relationship."

"That's a touching story, Jake, but I don't know why you decided to tell it to me now."

"There's a parallel to the story—you and me—with just one big difference, Kate. I care too much about you to be that liberal-minded. I'm *asking* you to stay, but we'd have to do it right. I'd want my ring on your finger, and all the promises that go with it."

"Jake! Are you . . . are you . . ."

"Proposing marriage," he finished for her. "If you give me a chance, maybe someday you'll learn to trust me and come to love me half as much as I love you."

"You love me?" Her tone was incredulous.

"With all my heart and soul. Will you marry me, Kate?"

"Marry you?" Her heart leapt with joy.

He reached out and traced her cheek with his fingers, and she stepped into his arms as if in a dream. "Oh, Jake." Kate breathed. "I've already trusted you with my life—that day we crossed the River of No Return. And as for learning to love you, well, I already love you so much I can't bear the thought of ever leaving you. I'd marry you in a minute—this very minute if you wanted me to, but Iron Man might not take the news too well."

"You won't be going back with them, sweetheart. Leave your father and Brian to me. I'm sure we can reach a gentleman's agreement." He bent down and placed a tender kiss on her forehead. "Everything will work out fine."

"Oh, Jake," Kate said again as she burrowed against his chest. "I think my heart was just waiting for you to walk

nto it. I'll never leave you. I love you now and I'll love you
orever."

Jake wasted no more time. He pulled her into his arms
nd kissed her deeply, binding their hearts and their prom-
ses. As Kate melted against him, giving herself up to the
earing heat of his kiss, she knew she was home. Home to
tay.

In the timber, the lone wolf cried, and this time an an-
wering call carried on the wind.

**Fifty red-blooded, white-hot, true-blue hunks
from every State in the Union!**

Look for MEN MADE IN AMERICA! Written by some
of our most poplar authors, these stories feature fifty of
the strongest, sexiest men, each from a different state in
the union!

Two titles available every other month at your favorite
retail outlet.

In January, look for:

DREAM COME TRUE by Ann Major (Florida)
WAY OF THE WILLOW by Linda Shaw (Georgia)

In March, look for:

TANGLED LIES by Anne Stuart (Hawaii)
ROGUE'S VALLEY by Kathleen Creighton (Idaho)

You won't be able to resist MEN MADE IN AMERICA!

NEW YORK TIMES Bestselling Author

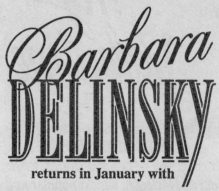

Barbara
DELINSKY

returns in January with

THE REAL THING

Stranded on an island off the coast of Maine,
Deirdre Joyce and Neil Hersey got the
solitude they so desperately craved—
but they also got each other, something they
hadn't expected. Nor had they expected
to be consumed by a desire so powerful
that the idea of living alone again was
unimaginable. A marrige of "convenience"
made sense—or did it?   B0B7

 HARLEQUIN®

My Valentine

1994

Celebrate the most romantic day of the year with
MY VALENTINE 1994
a collection of original stories, written by
four of Harlequin's most popular authors...

**MARGOT DALTON
MURIEL JENSEN
MARISA CARROLL
KAREN YOUNG**

*Available in February, wherever
Harlequin Books are sold.*

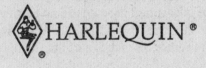

HARLEQUIN ®

VAL94

Relive the romance...
**Harlequin and Silhouette
are proud to present**

A program of collections of three complete novels by the most requested
authors with the most requested themes. Be sure to look for one volume each
month with three complete novels by top name authors.

In January: **WESTERN LOVING**   Susan Fox
                                          JoAnn Ross
                                          Barbara Kaye

Loving a cowboy is easy—taming him isn't!

In February: **LOVER, COME BACK!**   Diana Palmer
                                          Lisa Jackson
                                          Patricia Gardner Evans

It was over so long ago—yet now they're calling, "Lover, Come Back!"

In March: **TEMPERATURE RISING**   JoAnn Ross
                                          Tess Gerritsen
                                          Jacqueline Diamond

Falling in love—just what the doctor ordered!

Available at your favorite retail outlet.

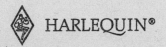

STOCK UP ON STOCKING STUFFERS
AND GET A FREE ROMANCE NOVEL

Collect all six STOCKING STUFFERS this December and receive a romance novel free—yours to enjoy when you have a few stolen moments to call your own. Once this special holiday season is over, take some time out to enjoy a longer-length romance novel from the romance experts—Harlequin and Silhouette—yours free when you collect all six proofs of purchase.

One proof of purchase can be found in the back pages of each STOLEN MOMENTS title this December.

To receive your gift, please fill out the information below and mail six (6) original proof-of-purchase coupons from December STOLEN MOMENTS titles, plus $1.00 for postage and handling (check or money order—do not send cash), payable to Harlequin Books, to: IN THE U.S.: P.O. Box 9071, Buffalo, NY, 14269-9071; IN CANADA: P.O. Box 604, Fort Erie, Ontario, L2A 5X3.

NAME: _____

ADDRESS: _____

_____

CITY: _____

STATE/PROVINCE: _____

ZIP/POSTAL CODE: _____

ONE PROOF OF PURCHASE   078 KBQ

Requests must be received by February 28, 1994.
Please allow 4–6 weeks after receipt of order for delivery.

HARLEQUIN ®   Silhouette®